THE NIGHT TURNER TRIBUNE

FIVE TALES OF TERROR

SAMANTHA JACKSON

LEE J. MINTER

Top Circle Publishing

Published by Top Circle 09/27/2018

ISBN 978-1-7327753-1-2

Library of Congress Control Number : 2018911584

Book layout by www.ebooklaunch.com

The Night Turner Tribune Five Tales of Terror, Samantha Jackson is an anthology of ghastly and terrifying stories written by the self-proclaimed rock star of horror Lee J. Minter himself, author of the best selling hit "In Sheep's Clothing" these five stories are designed to scare the living s#!t out of you. Make a hole and make it wide for the new master and self-proclaimed rock star of modern day horror and beyond aka mintboogie. Horror will never be the same, stay - tuned for the aftermath of carnage that his imagination leaves behind.

P.S. Before you pick it up, just remember to leave the lights on if you dare.

"If you only believe what you see, then the unseen remains protected to do as it please."

Mintboogie

Dedicated to family, friends, and fans here and abroad. Thanks for all your love and support, but most of all believing.

To my mother Shirley G. Minter with love & respect.

"I always had to be the opposite of what you wanted me to be because I had to be myself."

The Beginning

The large cockroach scurries along the floor of the dark room of the abandoned house in search of food and water amongst all the trash and other litter scattered about on its decrepit floors. Old and used drug paraphernalia brought in by addicts using the house as a drug den also decorate the interior of its numerous rooms floors.

The musty stench of decay and decadence hangs in the air of the abandoned house that was once inhabited by several generations of families, busy with the noise of births, birthdays, and even deaths. But that was the past this is now, soon the relic-like home in the not so good neighborhood, which people like to coin as the "Other side of town," will eventually be condemned by the City of New Orleans and razed like similar and other homes within the vicinity.

The cockroach now nibbles on an old piece of dried up pizza crust as its antennae flicker back and forth feeling and smelling out its environment, as another nocturnal creature now appears out of one of the numerous holes in the room's baseboards. It stands up on its hind legs sniffs the stale air with its pink nose and pinpoints the tasty little treat that the roach has discovered. The rat now runs along the floorboard in the direction of the cockroach for a two-in-one meal. The roach senses that it's in danger and dashes off quickly with a tiny piece of the pizza crust still in its mouth. The rat follows suit as it watches the roach run into one of the holes in the wall. The hole is small, but the rat pushes its head thru first now attempting to squeeze the rest of its body thru the wall hole, when something bites its nose, it lets out a squeak!

Another bite, squeak, then another, squeak! Something crawls into its mouth, large wet and slimy, the rats incisor-like teeth crush it spewing out its pus-like insides into its mouth, but then another one comes, trapping the first one in the rat's throat before its able to digest it completely, proceeded by another parasitic invader and so and so on.

The rat now has a horde of carnivorous invaders inside of its mouth and throat all fighting for space, cutting off its air supply as it struggles to breathe. The rodent's hairless tail does one last death wiggle before the rest of its body is snatched inside of the hole by its new found friends.

The large bait roach from its colony finishes up the last of the pizza crust and joins in for a more furry and tastier meal.

• • •

Two junkies now enter the abandoned home to shoot up their dope then afterward sleep off their high. They walk over to a corner of the house sit down and begin taking their drugs out. The male takes a clear plastic bag filled with what looks like white crystals out of his jacket as his female companion looks eagerly on.

It is cold inside of the abandoned house, but that is of little concern to them right now as she rubs her hands together in anticipation of her hit on the glass dope pipe. She watches as her boyfriend takes a long drag on the pipe, inhaling the vapors of the crystal meth inside. "Stop fucking around and let me hit that glass dick baby," she said. Her companion looks at her wild-eyed as he hands her over the pipe. "I wish you stop saying that kind of shit it makes me feel weird," he said.

She lit up the meth from the base of the pipe and took a long drag herself, inhaling the vapors and laughed. "You sure it's not all this good dope going to your brain making you paranoid babycakes?"

The both of them looked as if they had not slept or bathe for days.

The boyfriend scratched the open meth sores on the side of his face and his neck with his fingers.

"All I am saying "is" that if that (glass pipe) is a dick that would make me a "Homo" and I don't appreciate that shit," he said annoyed, as he snatches the drug paraphernalia out her hands. His companion eyes rolled back in her head as she laughs because she knew how to push his buttons.

"Calm down baby, it's not my fault you got skills," she said, as she proceeded to imitate performing fellatio with her mouth and hand while making slurping sounds.

"Fuck you," he said as he sucks on the glass meth pipe.

She smiled and looked at him coyly. "After I hit that glass dick homophobe." "You are one twisted fuck baby," he said with a grin on his face.

"Yeah, but you like it and this stinky stink," she said as rubs her groin and then begins to remove her clothes.

In the distance of the house, something watches them, in a corner, patiently, its eyes glowing ambiently in the darkness. Waiting its turn to bring the two of them back into a whole new, different kind of reality.

After they have their way with each other, it will have its way with them. And not in the nicest manner. Because on the wall above them as they engage in a drug-infused passion of intimacy, is the words written in dried blood "Beware of Izzy," A warning they should have taken more seriously.

THEY CALL IT IZZY

Original Story: by Lee J. Minter
Artwork by: Lee J. Minter

Chapter One

Sam felt as if she would never stop falling, but when she finally did. The dark lake water felt like she had fallen thru concrete before plummeting straight into its cold abyss.

The temperature in her body immediately started to drop once she hit the cold water that couldn't have been any warmer than thirty-six degrees. Sam knock-out by the fall begins to descend to the bottom of the lake inadvertently taking in gulps of lake water, she begins the process of drowning, when suddenly her eyes pop open into the hazy darkness. Instinct now kicks in as she held her breath and began swimming to the top of the lake. That's when she hears another splash, in the water and a growl.

The creature was still in pursuit of her and now swimming in her direction, its amber eyes eerily glowing luminescent in the dark. Sam had reached the top of the lake now but was still disorientated; from the fall.

As Sam struggles to get her balance and composure back, she suddenly heard someone calling out her name in the darkness of the night. All she had to do now Sam thought, was follow the direction of that person's voice, back to safety.

The earthy taste of the lake water filled her mouth and nostrils as she swam faster back towards the shoreline. Sam was almost there when suddenly something grabbed her ankle from behind and began pulling her back deeper into the lake, deeper into the darkness.

Sam screamed out in shock as she attempted to wiggle free of its vice-like grip, as its claws dug into the flesh of her ankles. She kicked one more time, and her foot made contact with its eye causing it to release her ankle. Sam took off swimming again and made it back to the shoreline. As she emerges out of the lake wet and cold, she could now see familiar faces although they were blurred waiting for her in the distance, it was her mom Gina, Sheriff Alvarez, and Cody Smith. "Sam watch out!" her mom shouted out. But it was too late as the big creature reached the shoreline behind her grabbing her by the collar. Sam turned around to face the creature and was met by the amber eyes of a killer by the eyes of a werewolf. Her scream was, just a gulp in her throat, which never came out not even when she woke up.

Sam wiped the cold sweat from her face as she looked over at the alarm clock on her nightstand that illuminated in red digital numbers, it was 4:00 am in the morning.

The sleeping pills that she had taken last night was not working, and she would have to ask her doctor for something stronger she concluded. Sam looked over beside her and noticed her boyfriend Brendon was still sound asleep. She rubbed her fingers thru his thick brown hair, staring at him in the dark. Brendon was always a sound sleeper she had noted, but of course, he did not have to deal with the visions and nightmares that had plagued her ever since she had left Harper Creek four years ago and taken a job in Chicago either. Sam could not help but harbor a jealous sense of envy of him in that respect, although she knew it was not his fault.

Sam quietly got out of the bed and made her way into the kitchen area of the spacious and comfy loft that she rented on the north side of Chicago in Lincoln Square.

She walked over to her kitchen counter and removed one of the small teacups that dangled off the rack mounted above the counter. Sam placed a small chamomile teabag that she had retrieved from a tea jar on the counter inside the cup, poured a small amount of water from a bottle into the cup and placed it inside her microwave. The microwave made a beeping sound as Sam pressed the buttons on its keypad to heat up the cup of tea.

The skyline of the Chicago river reflected thru her glass living room doors that gave access to an upper patio providing her with a spectacular view. Sam may have been a long way from home and the mountains of South Dakota, but in a way, she could not explain how she felt not oddly at all at home in Illinois.

The microwave beeped alerting Sam that her tea was now ready as she sat at the island bar in her kitchen in front of her laptop going over a news story that she was writing for her paper "The Night Turner Tribune." Sam felt something soft brush up against her leg as she got off the bar stool to get her tea. "Meow." It was a long-haired tabby she named Hi-Cee because of its orange coat. A rescue cat that she had adopted from the local shelter. She picked up Hi-Cee off the floor, cuddling the cat in her arms as she rubbed its fur.

"What's wrong boy? Are you in the mood for morning brunch," she said.

"Meow," answer Hi-Cee as it looked up at her with big green eyes that reminded her of bright green emeralds.

"Okay, boy I'll see what mommy can scrounge you up," Sam said, as she sat the cat down.

Hi-Cee bolted towards the glass patio doors as soon as its paws touch the loft's shiny wood floors.

Sam shook her head sideways as she watched her cat now scratching on the glass doors whining to get out. "Just like most men, you can't make up your mind what you want huh boy?" Sam said as she walked over to her patio doors to let Hi-Cee out for some fresh morning air.

The cat shot through the patio doors as Sam opened them and jumped up on one of the patio chairs. Sam took a sip of the hot tea that she had retrieved from the microwave that contrasted with the cool wind coming off the Chicago lakefront. A lone figure of someone standing across the street in front of her loft caught Sam eye. She gave a friendly wave to the stranger who's dark silhouette she could barely make out because of the morning mist still in the air, and the fact it was still dawn.

The stranger did not respond but just stood there staring in Sam's direction. Sam was sure whoever that person was, could see her and she now began to feel creeped out about their presence.

"Are you okay?" he asks, slightly startling her from behind. It was Brendon. Sam turned to face him and gave him a peck on the lips.

"Good Morning babe, I am fine. But maybe we should ask our friend across the street," Sam said.

"What are you talking about babe, there's no one there," Brendon said.

Sam quickly turned back around, Brendon was right there wasn't anyone across the street. Somehow her gazer had disappeared quietly into the streets of Lincoln Park, as quickly as they had appeared.

"I swear someone was there," Sam said confused.

"Hey, it could have been just a drunk or some kid playing a prank," Brendon said, trying to offer Sam some reasonable explanation.

"I guess so," Sam said still surveying the streets for her ominous gawker.

Brendon could still see that Sam was still slightly disturbed by the incident as he rubbed the side of her arm.

"Hey look, Sam, if you want me to go down and take a look around outside, I can do that babe," he offered.

Sam thought about his proposal for a moment, what was she doing to herself, to them? She thought. "Nah, that's okay babe, whoever it was is probably long gone by now, and it might be what you said it was," Sam's mouth stated, but her brain was telling her better. Anyway, she thought it was best now to change the subject.

"Hey, babe you want some tea?" Sam ask.

"Sure," Brendon said as he stared at Sam wondering how someone could still be so damn beautiful so early in the morning.

Brendon watched Sam as she walked over to the kitchen in his shirt to make him some tea, he loved how his shirt seemed to hug her ass, the creases in the shirt moving symmetrically with every stride her long legs took towards the kitchen. How did he get so damn lucky he wonders? As he watched Sam make his tea.

"Cream and sugar?"

"Just sugar," Brendon responded.

But if anyone were to ask Sam she would have said; she was the lucky one. When the two first met thru mutual friends, Sam had to admit to herself it was not exactly "love" at first sight for either one of them, but they knew it was something there between them, a spark that could maybe become a flame or an explosion. His first impression of Sam was that she was tough and driven and spoke her mind. And boy, was he right on the money about the third assumption.

He was impressed that she had come down to a tough city like Chicago to pursue her career in journalism if you could survive on the streets of Chicago his attitude was you could survive anywhere. He should know, being that he was a war veteran of Desert Storm and now a two-year rookie officer on the Chicago Police Department who was up against a different kind of war that now infested the streets of the City most people still knew affably as "Shy-town."

But Brendon Crust was different because every decision he had made during his adult life was by choice, not a necessity. At least in the aspect that most people make decisions in their lives. Because, unlike most cops on "the job" he had been born into a life of privilege, in Chicago's Old Town where million dollar homes were about as common as caviar were as an appetizer and cocaine was as Chanel.

His father Jonathan Crust was a well-known bigwig and shot caller in the world of finance in Chicago. A Banker by trade he had founded his own company Crust Holdings LLC. Which had its stake in real estate, restaurants, entertainment and anything else that the Senior Crust thought could generate him a buck or two? There had even been some rumors of mafia ties associated with some of his more lucrative business dealings.

Brendon Crust meanwhile had observed his father's wheeling and dealing from afar, and although he had been his son in name and birthright, he had not been the prodigy son that his father expected and had not displayed his father's interest or his passion for chasing dead presidents stamp on mint green paper.

If one were to ask, he would say, Brendon was more like his mother, Brendon's mom Sarah, which he felt was an inherent weakness, which his son possessed.

That the boy that was now a man gave a damn too much about trying to make sure that the underdogs and those members of society that did not have the wealth and privilege he had came from did not get screwed. Yes, it was a noble way of looking at the world, his father agreed, just not a realistic view of how things were in the concrete jungle he had to survive in. On the other hand, Senior Crust viewed the world thru a different set of binoculars; whereas in this world it was survival of the fittest to him plain and simple.

As they both sat at the island bar sipping on tea, Brendon looked gazingly into Sam's eyes.

"Having those nightmares again I take it?" he asks concerned.

"Damn he's perceptive," Sam thought before she answered.

"Yeah, they come, and they go," Sam replied, trying not to sound too concern herself about the matter because the last thing she wanted was Brendon to worry about her while he was out there on some of the dangerous streets of Chicago trying to do his job as a police officer.

She wanted him to stay sharp and focus.

"Sam, can I ask you a question?" Brendon asks as he takes another sip of his tea.

"Sure," Sam said.

"Everyone knows, that the Night turner Tribune is responsible for some pretty (I hope no offense taken) outrageous stories, and I was wondering as talented as you are why you are not with a more..." Brendon thought it was best for him to stop there.

"Reputable paper," Sam interjected, finishing his thought.

"The only thing I can tell you babe is because of that factor alone is why I wake up every day ready to take on this world because, in this crazy job of mine, I never know what to expect," Sam said.

"I can relate to that," Brendon said with a smile.

Sam was now between Brendon's legs as she held his face in her hands and gently kissed him on the lips.

"Don't worry about me so much babe, I am a tough bitch!" she said.

"So I've heard," Brendon acknowledge.

Sam put her hands between Brendon's legs and begin to massage his crotch.

"That means I won't break," she leaned forward and whispered in his ear softly.

Brendon loved the way Sam smelled in the early morning hours when they made love to each other even more he loved how her flower budded and tasted in his mouth.

"I'll go easy on you," Sam said, as she looked into Brendon's eyes.

"Promise?" he said.

"Nope," Sam answered back with a smile as she took Brendon by the hand and led him into the bedroom.

Chapter Two

Avery Denton, the Night Turner Tribune's Editor & Chief was on the phone engaged in a heated conversation with someone on the other end when Sam, knocked on his office door to enter. He saw her thru the glass pane in his door that had his name and title on it and waved her inside of his office.

"All I am asking of you is that you make sure that when my reporter gets down there, you keep her in the loop, agreed? Good, I'll keep in touch." Denton hung up the phone.

"Jerk." He muttered, and then he looked up at Sam as if he had almost forgotten that she was standing there.

"Good Morning Chief, should I come back at another time?" Sam said with an awkward look on her face.

"No, not at all." Her boss said as he pressed his vest down with his hands. "Please have a seat, Sam, I think I have a helluva assignment for you," he said.

Sam looked at him confused.

"But Chief I am already working on the Langelli case."

"Maria Langelli the exorcism case, I know Sam, but we are going to have to put that on hold for now,"

Denton stressed, much to the disappointment of Sam. He knew that she had been working long and hard on the Langelli case, but it seemed like these days demonic possession cases were a dime a dozen. What Denton felt was that his paper needed something fresher to bring up its readership numbers and this next story might be the magna cum laude to do just that.

" You know you're one of my best reporters Sam, that's why I am asking you to put the Langelli case on hold because we have bigger fish to fry," he said confidently.

"How big?" Sam asked her curiosity now peeked. "Magna Cum Laude big," Denton said with a poker face. "Okay, chief I am all ears where's the action?" Sam said.

"New Orleans, I need you to fly out tonight."

"Lousiana, what am I looking into down there?"

"I have information thru a reliable source Sam, that there's been a string of strange homicides down there in New Orleans, and rumor has it that some of the locals believe the murders were not committed by anything or anyone human but something not of this world," Denton said.

"Such as?" Sam asked.

"Brace yourself, for this one. A demon."

"Interesting Chief, and does this demon have a name?" Sam asked.

Denton leaned back in his chair with his hands folded in his lap, studying Sam's face. "Funny that you asked Sam, but it might," he said.

"Well, what is it?"

"Well, according to our sources at each crime scene they found 'Beware of Izzy' scrawled on the wall in blood," Denton answered.

"How very Manson," Sam said.

"I know," he agreed.

She had absorbed everything her boss had just told her; but she knew that she could be chasing a demon of the two-legged kind, just as well as one of the super-natural.

"One more thing, Sam."

"What's that Chief?"

"Be careful."

Sam winked her eye at her boss.

"Always," she said as she exited his office.

"That's what I am worried about," he said to himself shaking his head as he watches Samantha leave out of his office.

Chapter Three

Sam's flight from Chicago O' Hare to Louis Armstrong New Orleans International Airport had finally arrived two and a half hours on its schedule. Sam now made her way briskly thru the busy hub of the airport after collecting her luggage from the baggage claim the only thing she wanted now after her two-and-a-half-hour flight in was a hot shower and a soft bed in a comfortable hotel room.

As Sam now rolled her luggage behind her, she visually scanned the airport lobby area for a liaison by the name of Tracy Leaumont that her newspaper agency had arranged to meet her there at the airport and provide any assistance that she needed during her time in New Orleans.

Sam looked thru the crowd of airport pedestrians at the signs with the names printed on them held up by chauffeurs and strangers, until her eyes came to one that said, *Sam* on it. Sam waved over to the stranger that held the small sign in his hands with her name printed on it catching his attention, as their eyes locked on each other. He smiled back at her as he headed over to assist her with her luggage and introduce himself to Sam.

"Welcome to New Orleans, Ms. Jackson. I am Tracy Leaumont," he said.

"Nice to meet you, Tracy, you may call me Sam by the way," she said, shaking as his hand.

Her liaison was not what Sam was expecting; he was a very attractive young man around her age, tall, dark and handsome with a winning smile. And although Brendon was no slouch, she doubted if he would approve of a liaison to her that looks like he had just stepped off the cover of a men's Vogue magazine. She wondered if Denton was unintentionally setting her up.

"May I?" Tracy asked as he looked at one of her luggage's on wheels.

"Thanks, be my guest, " Sam said, a gentleman she thought to herself.

Tracy took hold of one of Sam's luggage by the handle. "This way to the garage," he pointed.

"You lead I'll follow," Sam said grateful for his help.

"I know you must be very tired after your flight in, what hotel are you staying in?"

"The Daupont Orleans Hotel," Sam answered.

"Oh, I know that one, it's a very nice hotel in the French Quarter."

"Do tell," Sam said, as they now loaded her luggage in the trunk of Tracy's car.

"Do tell," Tracy repeated with a smile and a wink, as he opened Sam's car door for her.

Sam was thankful that the drive from the airport to the hotel took less than thirty-five minutes as she graciously took in the sights, sounds, and smells, of New Orleans. It wasn't long before they had arrived in the French quarter section of the city, the Creole cottages and Historical mansions pop out at Sam, giving her the feeling that she had stepped back into a time machine and was viewing another era of history in Lousiana's past good and bad.

As they pulled up in front of the Daupont Orleans Hotel Guest Parking, Sam took in the sight of the hotel.

She noticed It was a quaint and elegant French colonial-styled building painted in a yellow pastel. Similar to the other beautiful French or Spanish colonial buildings that adjoined it and decorated the quarter.

"Here we are," Tracy said as he exited the vehicle to help Sam unload her luggage.

"Thanks, for the ride Tracy," Sam said as she gathers up her luggage out of the trunk of his car.

"Would you like to grab a couple of drinks after you check in?" Tracy asked with a smile, as he closed the trunk of his car down.

"I am really, tired Tracy, so I am going to have to take a rain check tonight, but how about brunch tomorrow, and we can start fresh."

"Sounds good, I'll see you in the morning," Tracy said.

Sam followed his eyes towards her luggage, she did not want to appear rude, but she was butt ass tired and ready to hit the sack.

"I'll take it from here, thanks."

"Goodnight," Tracy said, before he smiled, and waved goodbye.

"Thanks again, same to you," Sam said.

Tracy stopped at his car door before he got in and watched as Sam headed into the hotel lobby, he had to admit to himself she wasn't what he was expecting. Denton never told him that the reporter he was sending was young, beautiful and "well" Sam.

Sam noted that the inside of the Daupont Orleans Hotel was no disappointment either. It was well lit and furnished with a touch of "Creole class" one could say.

She walked up to the registration desk in the lobby that was being manned by one Daupont employee to check in.

"Good evening, how may I help you?" the employee said as Sam caught her attention.

"Good evening, I have reservations here," she said as she handed the receptionist her driver license and corporate card.

Sam watched as the receptionist took her documents and pulled her reservations up on the computer in front of her.

"Ah' here you are Ms. Jackson," she said in a cheerful voice, as she handed Sam back over her documents.

"Welcome to New Orleans."

"Thank you," Sam said.

"Here you go."

The receptionist handed Sam two access key cards for her room.

"Enjoy your stay with us, Ms. Jackson," said that cheerful voice again.

"I'll try," Sam said with a smile, that hid the fact that her tired body was in desperate need of a hot bath and a soft bed.

Her brain, now told her it was time for her to make a bee-line to her hotel room and fall out on her bed before the very-polite receptionist decided to exchange more pleasantries to make her feel right at home.

Sam inserted one of the key cards into the door's card lock, a clicking sound emitted from the hotel door card lock letting her know the door was now unlocked.

She turned the door's handle and entered the nicely decorated hotel room with her luggage in tow, Sam walked over to the hotel bed and dropped one of her bags on onto it. She watched the bag sink into the bed with envy.

Sam then unzipped the bag and took out her laptop, and it's accessories and set all of it up on a nearby desk table in the room. Just as she was finishing up, she suddenly heard a knock on her hotel door. Who could it be she thought? "Room service," said the voice on the other side of the door. "Just a minute," Sam said as she made her way to the door.

Sam looked thru the peephole on the door, thru the hole she could see room service dressed neatly in a similar uniform to the front desk receptionist. Sam unlocked and opened the door. She did not recall ordering anything? She thought.

"Good evening Ms. Jackson, I have a bottle of Pinot noir for you," room service said pleasantly with a smile. Sam looked at the bottle of wine inside the ice bucket on a small silver cart next to a wine glass, and a plate of appetizers. "Good evening, "wow" it looks delicious, but I believe there's been a mistake," she said.

The employee smiled and looked at her room number on the wall as if he knew something that she did not.

" You are Samantha Jackson?" He asked.

"Yes," Sam answered back. The employee looked at his notepad. "Right person, and it has already been taking care of Ms. Jackson," he said.

"May I?" he added.

"Sure," said Sam as she allowed him to enter with the cart.

"Thank you," Sam said as she handed him a tip. The employee nodded his head in appreciation.

"Thank you, Ms. Jackson, and have a very good night."

"Same to you," Sam responded.

"By the way Ms. Jackson, I hope you don't find this inappropriate to ask?" he said with hesitation in his voice.

"Go ahead," Sam said anticipating the question.

"You wouldn't be Samantha Jackson, the writer, at The Night Turner Tribune?" he said nervously.

"Yes, guilty as charged," Sam said with a smile she manages to put on her face to put him at ease.

"Wow, I read all your stuff, Ms. Jackson, you're like a legend in the world of paranormal," he said excitedly. Sam rolled her eyes.

"I don't think I am that old or seasoned, but I am flattered by the compliment, nevertheless, so thanks."

"You're welcome, keep up the good work Ms. Jackson, the world need's to know what's out there."

Sam closed the door behind him. I don't know if the world is ready for that she thought, as she walked over to the wine cart and lifted up the little card attached to the bottle of Pinot noir. *"Welcome to New Orleans, enjoy! Tracy Leaumont.*

The card attached to the bottle of red wine fell out of Sam's hand, as she stared off into the distance of the room.

The room begins to take another shape of its own as if she was looking thru a Kaleidoscope of revolving colors, spinning around in her brain. A room that is now metamorphosing into a thing of another dimension.

All of the light in the room now starts to fade away as Sam finds herself falling thru the darkness, frozen in space and time as she stares into an abyss of nothingness. The room now starts to allow light to get thru, to penetrate the darkness.

The smell of candles, hang in the damp air, accompanied by the smell of decay and rot. As more light comes thru, Sam's vision becomes clearer, less obscure. She can now see that she is no longer in the fancy room of the Daupont hotel, she is in somebody's basement.

The chains and shackles attached to the basement walls catch Sam's eyes, as she heads slowly over to them. For some odd reason, she cannot explain, she feels a strange familiarity with those shackles of bondage.

The closer she gets to them she can now see that they are dripping with blood, fresh blood. Sam stops. What was that? She can now hear someone or something else entering the basement walking down its creaking steps, creak, creak, creak. It is getting closer and closer to her.

Sam's mind is now racing because she wants to run, but there is no place to run too. She wants to hide, but there is no place to hide but underneath the concrete floor permanently.

The thing has now descended the basement stairs; she can see that it is massive in its size and weight. It stares at her silently and malevolently waiting for her to make a move, any move. Its whole being is covered in shadowy darkness.

A cold chill runs thru Sam's body "Who are you?" Silence. "What do you want?" No answer, as the creature takes a step closer to her in the barely breathable confines of the basement. Sam takes a step back in synchronicity with the creature's step forward. Her eyes go to the glistening dagger in its left hand.

"Who are you dammit?" Sam screams out one more time, as her eyes now go to the various weapons mounted on the basement's wall above a Baphomet statue. If she can reach one of those weapons she reasons, maybe she will have a chance to make it past the behemoth and out of this dirty hell hole.

"You are Sam," the creature said, a creature that was more beast than man. It's stringy hair from its head hung in front of its face-obscuring Sam from visually making out anything "fathomably human" behind its greasy, and dirty tresses.

"Yes asshole, I am Sam, and who in the fuck are you?" Sam shouted out defiantly.

"I have many names; some people call me The Butcher, The Highway Strangler, The Creeper, I like *The Slayer* personally," the creature said in a diabolical tone. Sam eyes quickly shot back over at the wall of mounted weapons; one of the weapons was an ancient ax its wooden handle wrapped in twine.

"You should not have come back here Sam; you should have stayed away," the creature said as it advanced closer towards Sam.

"Fuck you!" Sam shouted out as she lunged herself towards the wall, grabbing the ax off its hooks. No sooner than when she righted herself back on her feet the creature is almost upon her with the blade in its hand. Sam swings the ax with all of the strength in her body.

As the sharp-edged blade of the ax makes contact with the creature's neck, it slices thru cartilage and bone. The creature lets out a bloody scream and stumbles back. Its neck is now barely attached to its shoulders. It fights to maintain its balance as it wobbles from side to side.

"Slayer my ass," Sam said. The creature than charges at Sam wobbly neck and all, as she swiftly dealt the last fatal blow to its neck, decapitating its head from its body.

Sam watched as the head with the greasy, stringy hair roll onto the floor, separated from its body. It's soulless black eye's now staring up at her.

It was a twisted face with those black pupils that was almost barely human to her, but she recognized that face despite its inhumanness. That face belongs to a man named Elwood Holmes.

The face smiles at her and winks one of its souless eyes. "What the fuck?" Sam said, as she reactively jumps back and comes down on the head with the ax splitting it in half.

That is when she notices a beeping noise. Sam looks up and sees the red led lights pulsating in sync with the beeps all around her. That is when it hits her, the fucking place is rigged and is about to blow-up. A hand suddenly reaches out and grab her by the ankle. It's the headless body of Elwood Holmes. "Nooooo!" Sam screams out while looking down at the body as she struggles to break free.

She begins hacking at the headless body's wrist with the ax until its hand that has her ankle is no longer attached to its arm. "Fuck you, Elwood," Sam said defiantly again as she breaks free, kicking the hand across the floor. The beeping stops. Sam looks up at the ceiling in the basement. "Noooooo!" she screams out again, but it's too late.

The explosion, disintegrates her body and the one on the floor, next to her, tossing her into nothingness again, into darkness.

CHAPTER FOUR

Beep-beep-tap. Sam hit the silence button on the chirping alarm clock on her nightstand, as she woke up from the nightmare that she had just had.

She rubbed the sleep out of her eyes as she looked over at the half glass of red wine on the metal cart. She did not remember pouring it and she damn sure didn't remember having any of it last night. But she must have? She thought. Because there it set on the cart half-full reminding her of last night and of course, she reasoned the bottle did not pour itself into the wine glass.

Sam looked over at the desk clock again; it said 6:00 am. "Time to rise and shine," she said to herself, as she pulled the blanket away and from off of her, exiting the bed, and making her way to the bathroom that was just a few steps away. She had promised Tracy that she would meet him for a light breakfast this morning to go over the details of the homicides that had happened in the lower ninth ward of New Orleans. One of the areas that were hit hard by Hurricane Katrina.

The lower ninth ward was still struggling to get back on its feet despite being slated by the government for funding and redevelopment.

A neighborhood that was predominately inhabited by African Americans that was now starting to see an influx of white millennials along with the new development that most of the residents viewed as gentrification to inevitably push them out. The question no one appeared to be asking is where they would go? Or could it be simply that those with vested interest and money did not care about people that were there long ago, before the levees ever broke and were now considered disenfranchised and disconnected by the struggles of poverty, to whatever faith those with the power, money, and vision had in store for them?

The New, New Orleans some were calling it. To Izzy, it was all the same. Her favorite colors used to be pink and blue; she used to love to laugh and play. No more of that. Now all she sees is red and darkness, and it makes her angry, very angry.

The small café that Tracy had chosen for him and Sam to have breakfast in the French Quarter was bristling with activity from a mixture of locals and tourist. The sound of dishes clanging and people talking filled the air, as they both sat across from each other at a small bistro table dining on a breakfast of Bananas Foster Belgian Waffles and a side order of Praline bacon, that Sam could not help with every bite fine sinfully delicious.

Sam, could feel Tracy's eye's on her as she bit into her bacon. She wonders what he is thinking of all of this, what he is thinking of her? "Thank you for the gift last night, the wine was a delicious nightcap," Sam said, appreciatively.

"You're welcome Sam; I am glad that you enjoyed the Pinot, it was my way of saying no hard feelings for rejecting my offer to have a drink with me last night," Tracy said. Sam raised an eyebrow at this comment and was about to say something when Tracy cut her off. "Just kidding," he said with a smile that Sam noticed lit up his distractingly handsome face even more. "I hope not," Sam replied with a smile to match his.

Sam now watched as Tracy's expression on his face suddenly went from gleefulness to confusion. "Just kidding," she said with a smile. Tracy shook his finger at Sam while laughing. "You almost had me."

"That will teach you not to let your guards down," Sam said.

"With you?" Tracy asked. "With everything," Sam answer, as she took a sip of her coffee.

Tracy looked at the woman that sat before him even more curiously now, just as he had thought there was more to her than meets the eye.

"I hate to mix pleasure with business, but what can you tell me about the recent deaths in the ninth ward Tracy?" Sam asked.

Tracy shifted uncomfortably in his seat now; Sam could detect a change of tone in his voice a tone of uneasiness.

"What can I say, Sam? Other than I know that these recent deaths are homicides, and they're some of the most brutal and strangest homicide scenes I have seen yet. And trust me I have seen some strange shit happen down here."

"But don't take my word for it, see it for yourself," he said, as he handed Sam a manilla envelope out of the messenger bag that hung on his chair beside him.

Tracy watched Sam's face as she pulled the photos out of the manilla envelope studying each one carefully.

He was quite surprised at how she seems to look at them with an expression on her face that did not convey any sense of what she was feeling. He knew what the photo's portrayed and how shocking and disturbing they could appear to anyone that viewed them. But unknown to him, Sam was not just anyone. She had seen far gruesome things in her life and profession. And thus, she had learned to develop an emotional disconnect when necessary, to make a clearer assessment of the cases she was reporting and writing about. One of the photos showed a possible suicide or homicide victim pick your choice, hanging from the rafters of an old house. The other photo was of a male impaled by a beam thru the chest. The horrid look on his face told Sam he never saw his death coming.

The question then to Sam was who and what was behind these deaths? The third photo though was the one she found the most disturbing and was of a young girl that couldn't have been any older than ten or twelve, and it was obvious by the photo evil and unspeakable things had been done to the child. Sam could also tell by the photo, that it appeared that the killer had staged the girl's body and crime scene to fit their twisted fantasy. Sam also noticed that the one thing that all these victims appeared to have in common was, the deplorable conditions that they had died in -

abandoned homes, she presumed in the lower ninth ward.

Sam stuffed the photos back into the envelope and handed it back to Tracy. "The child, how is she related to the two other victims?" Sam asked. Tracy leaned back in his chair rubbing his chin. "She's not, she was the first," he answered solemnly.

"Any leads on who her killer might be and do you think their's a connection?"

"I don't know? The police are just as stumped as they are about the other two homicides," Tracy said.

"Not good for the community with a monster like that still walking around out there looking for its next victim," Sam said.

"You think?" Tracy said. Sam ignored the reply.

"The two adult victims what's the story on them?" Sam wanted to know.

Tracy now held both of his hands together in a triangle formation. "I don't know if you can classify those two as victims with the history they had between them, or was it more like karma's time to collect," Tracy rebuttal.

"What do you mean?" Sam said.

"This," Tracy said, as he handed Sam a few pages of paper with their arrest record and history printed on it.

Tracy was right; Sam thought as she viewed their rap sheet, these two had been far from upstanding citizens of their community. Burglary, Narcotics, Child Abuse, and a conviction each of Criminal Sexual Conduct first degree against a minor under sixteen years of age.

These two fuck up's Sam could see were just like that man she heard about in Brunsdale Fargo, that slather barbecue sauce on his pecker for a joke and dangle it over a hungry pit bulls mouth. Bad shit was bound to happen eventually when stupidity met faith.

The legal system Sam knew was, unfortunately, a revolving door that allowed freaks like this to slip thru the cracks way too often. Tracy was right; the chickens had come home to roost.

"I think I'll pass on the dessert," Sam said as she handed Tracy back the police file.

"I figured you would," Tracy said as he took the file from Sam and placed it back in his messenger bag.

Sam looked around the Café and noticed the breakfast crowd was starting to wind down as customers were beginning to leave. "May I ask, how did you obtain this information?" Sam said curiously.

"Let's just say it's good to know the right people in this town, and when you look out for them, they don't mind looking out for you," Tracy said with a grin on his face. "I see and are you one of those right people?"

"I could be," Tracy answered with a glint in his eyes. "Are you ready to see another side of New Orleans?" "I thought you'd never ask?" Sam said. Sam then raised her hand to get the attention of their waiter. "Check, please," she requested. The waiter nodded his head in acknowledgment. After only a few seconds had passed by he returned with the check. Sam quickly took the bill from the waiter went over it just as quickly and paid it and the tip.

"Wine's on you; breakfast is on me," she said To Tracy.

"Thanks, big spender," Tracy said. "All on the company's dime," Sam replied with a wink as both of them then rose from the table gather up their bags and exited the Café into the bright sunlight and cool morning air filled with the sounds and smells of the French Quarter.

The drive down to the lower ninth ward took longer than Sam had expected due to the morning traffic congestion but eventually her and her liaison Tracy arrived in a neighborhood that she could see had probably long suffered economic dispair before Hurricane Katrina had unleashed its wrath and devastation on the area.

Sam could not help but feel a tinge of guilt as she viewed the dilapidated homes and overgrown lots that her occupational and educational status afforded her the luxury of a higher standard of living. But there was another thing that she knew in her heart as well, that guilt is not what this neighborhood and the residents needed. They needed action and support from their local government agencies and representatives to make a true comeback to stability and recovery. Sam could only imagine with a sigh as she looked on that the red tape of bureaucracy here was probably as long as the Industrial Canal, a shipping channel that cut off the lower ninth ward from the rest of New Orleans. Tracy pulled the car in front of one of the many abandoned-looking homes in a neighborhood, that had an almost war zone look to it.

As they both exited the vehicle, Sam looked around the neighborhood for a sign of life; there was none. "Is this where the last homicides happen?" Sam asked

Tracy as she adjusted her Nikon camera that hung by a strap around her neck. "It is and a lot more I am sure," Tracy said looking in the direction of the old house.

A cool breeze swept by, blowing debris in the direction of their feet, as they now made their way towards the abandoned house that they could now see had no trespass and condemned signs taped on the front of its boarded-up windows. A stream of yellow crime scene tape hung out the crack of the dilapidated door fluttering whenever a cool breeze blew by.

"Nice digs," Tracy said sarcastically. Sam looked at him, "You think?" The both of them was now standing on the front porch of the two-story home. The front door opened up with a creak and little resistance as Tracy tugged at it. "Watch your step, Sam," he said as they both entered the house. Despite being morning and daylight outside it was very dark inside of the house with only shimmers of light seeping thru the cracks and crevices of its walls and boarded up windows. "It stinks in here," Tracy said. "Death usually does," Sam retorted. Tracy reaches into his messenger bag and pulls out the yellow manilla envelope. He then opens it up and pulls out some of the homicide photos of the recently deceased couple that had the misfortune of attempting to use this place to get high and slap monkeys (sex). Sam aims a small led pen flashlight on the photos then back on the cracked, dirty walls of the room.

She has now verified the room they're standing in matches one of the photos that Tracy is holding in his hand.

"Wow look at this," Sam said as the lumens from the penlight illuminated the words sprawled out on the wall in front of them.

"Beware of Izzy!"

"Is that blood or paint?" Tracy said as he stared at the warning written in letters that appeared to be oozing down the wall. Tracy walked up to the wall closer. "Wait a minute is that fresh blood?" he said, upon closer inspection of the wall. The warning to him seemed to pulsate with a life of its own.

Click, click, flash. Sam took a picture of the wall and the warning. Tracy reached out to touch the warning, to see if the letters were blood, fresh blood. Bang, Clanggg! "What the fuck?" Tracy blurted out. The noise stopping him in his tracks.

"Don't!" Sam screamed out.

"Are you two kids having fun?" a voice said coming out of nowhere. Two men in suits and ties stood in the corridor behind them. It was no mistaking what they were - cops. "I guess you two don't know what the words no trespass mean?" said the older of the two that had initially addressed them.

"We do, Detective Devereaux, but we weren't expecting you so soon, short line at the donut shop?" Tracy said.

Sam felt a sense of relief come over her, that Tracy knew these two.

"Fuck you," the detective responded. A smirk came over the younger cop's face. "Tracy I didn't know she was your type," he said. Tracy winked at him. "She's not; I like my men with some oink in them." "And may I ask who do we have the pleasure of meeting in such palatial surroundings?" The older cop said, turning his attention to Sam.

"Oh hi, I am Samantha Jackson, from the Night Turner Tribune." "Another reporter huh?" said the younger cop.

"Glad to meet you too sunshine," Sam replied.

The older cop laughed. "Yeah, we got a report of suspicious activity out here, are you two aware that this was a recent crime scene?" Devereaux ask. "No, we just came in here to smoke a little crack," Tracy answered.

"Well you pick the right place," Devereaux said.

The younger detective shook his head sideways in disapproval. Tracy ignored him. He turned his attention to Sam. "Where are you from Ms. Jackson?" "Chicago, sunshine." Devereaux chuckled. His partner Canty, unfortunately, did not share his same sense of humor.

"Detective Canty," he said flatly, rolling his eyes in his head to express his annoyance. "Gotcha," Sam said, hoping that her conciliatory acknowledgment might loosen the proverbial stick stuck up in Canty's ass.

Sam, curiously looked back over at the strange writing on the wall in what appeared to be an ominous warning to trespassers.

"Anyone knows who Izzy is and why we should beware?" she asked.

Detective Devereaux turned in the direction to face the wall and studied the cryptic message scrawled on its surface. "Oh, that? Izzy was the nickname of the little girl that was murder here." "Isabella?" Tracy said.

"Yes, Mulder," Canty said sarcastically, referencing the fictional character of the X-files. "But why would someone write her nickname up on this wall as a warning?" Sam inquired.

"Because not only are the locals poor in this community Sam, they are also very superstitious, and they believe the spirit of that little girl is still haunting this place," Devereaux said. "For what?" Sam asked. "Lady, are you always this persistent?" Canty interjected. "If I was a man, would you ask me like that?" Sam said, with a glance that told Detective Canty he did not want to go there. Lucky for him, he didn't.

Devereaux shook his head sideways and chuckled again.

"I like her Tracy; she's a tough cookie," Devereaux said. "You meant tough bitch," Sam said. "If I may respectfully oblige," Devereaux said with a smile. Canty looked on with that smirk on his face. "Now the answer to your question Ms. Jackson, why do the residents around here think that poor little-deceased girl is haunting this shitty place?"

"That might be a question that you best ask them."

"Now if you don't have any more questions for my partner and me I think we can find some real police work to attend to."

"Like a beignet with your name on it," Tracy said, condescendingly.

"Don't let the door hit you in your sweet ass on the way out," Canty said.

"I am not worried as long as you're watching it, big boy," Tracy said, with a wink. Detective Canty raised both of his middle fingers to Tracy on his way out.

Tracy threw up the call me sign to Canty with a grin on his face as he watches both men leave.

"Did I miss something?" Sam asked. "Not much, Devereaux is just trying to do enough to make his pension, his partner Canty has got repressed sexual feelings for me and doesn't know how to deal with them."

"Wow, I wasn't expecting all of that," Sam said. "Hey, Ms. Nosy you asked, I answered," Tracy pointed out. "Fair enough, and since Detective Devereaux was intentionally being evasive and would not answer my question, I guess that leaves us little choice but to ask around the neighborhood about why the spirit of this little girl is haunting this house?." Tracy was now taken aback by what Sam had just proposed. He had to ask himself, was she crazier than he thought she was? Or just willing to take more risk than he was at this time.

"That's a real noble idea Sam, but you did you happen to see the surrounding neighborhood when we were driving up?"

"It's not exactly the Taj Mahal," Tracy pointed out.

"Get out! And don't return!" a booming voice commands them, startling them both. Sam and Tracy turn in the direction of the house that they thought they heard the ominous warning, they see no one.

"Hey is there anyone else in here?" Sam shouted out.

Silence, dead silence.

"Man that was some Scooby Doo shit," Sam said.

Tracy turns towards Sam; his face says it all, now might be a good time to leave.

Chapter Five

As Sam and Tracy, both exits the dilapidated house, the sunshine is almost blinding to them as they step out into the daylight. The smell of cool fresh air permeates their nostrils.

A familiar booming voice from a disheveled looking stranger greets them again. *"Get out! And don't return,"* he warns them again.

"You are not a ghost after all," Tracy says, with a sense of relief to the stranger.

"No more of a ghost than you two are," he answers back, in a gruff voice.

As they approach the stranger closer, Sam greets him politely. "Hello, my name is Sam, and this is Tracy, we are doing a story on the murders that occurred here in this house." Sam extends her hand to shake his; he does not acknowledge it, leaving it drifting in the air untouched, as he looks them both over suspiciously.

"I don't give a tater's ass if your names are Puss n' bootie,s you don't need to be snooping around these parts," he barked out firmly.

"Furthermore her family needs to mourn that child in peace," he added, scratching his stubble chin.

"And we couldn't agree with you more, but if our report on what happened to that innocent little girl, moves one person to come forward and give some evidence, that might be crucial to catching a child killer Mister…" Sam paused, hoping that the eccentric figure before them would take the bait. "Rufus," he said. There it was, she now had a name to go with their antagonist. She gladly then finished her question to him.

"Rufus, don't you think it would be worth it?"

Their new hobo-like friend scratched his stubble chin again, looking downward at the ground as he contemplated what Sam had just told him. Tracy watched him closely with guarded eyes.

"Maybe you're right; maybe you're wrong," he answers back.

It wasn't the answer that Sam was looking for, but at least in its apparent ambiguousness, it was a start. Sam and Tracy watched as Rufus removed a bottle of something with a clear liquid in it and took a long swig of it. To their surprise, he offers them some of its contents. They politely decline.

"Mr. Rufus, did you know that little girl?" Tracy asked.

Rufus wiped his lips off with the back of his hand and placed his bottle back into his tattered coat pocket. "Yeah, everyone did, sweet little girl, but not anymore," he said.

Sam could now smell the scent of alcohol coming from his breath.

"What do you mean by not anymore?" Sam asked.

Rufus looked nervously at Tracy back to Sam. "Word has it that she has come back from the dead for revenge, but the only thing is, what came back is not her, it's something else," he said. "*What is it?*" Sam pressed on. Rufus' eyes begin to widen even more as if he had been struck by a bolt of lighting. He then begins to tremble, as if something had now taken hold of him.

"What is it?" Sam shouted out. The sound of her voice seemed to snap him out of his catatonic spell.

"Izzy!" he shouted back with as much vigor as he did in his earlier forewarning to them. "Isabella," Sam said softly. "No Izzy, not the same," Rufus said.

"look I've said too much already, I gots to go, and I advise yall to do the same and never come back," he warned.

Sam reached into her jacket pocket and pulled out a twenty dollar bill and offered it to Rufus. He looked at it discriminately. "What is that? I can't spend that in hell," he said, offensively.

His eyes went back to the twenty dollar bill Sam still held out to him.

"But on second thought, *Jojo's Beer and Wine* will accept it," he said, snatching the twenty dollar bill rudely from Sam's hand.

Tracy watched on with that guarded look still in his eyes. "Thank you for the information, Mr. Rufus," Sam said, as they watched him begin to leave.

Rufus stopped in his tracks and turned around slowly at them. "Don't thank me; only three outcomes can come from this," he shouted back at them.

"And what's that?" Tracy shouted back.

"You catch the killer or meet the devil," Rufus said, as he began to walk away again.

"Wait, what's the third outcome?" Sam shouted out.

Rufus stopped again and looked back at them both, but this time Sam could see it was something different in his face, his eyes.

"Both," he said.

Tracy turns to Sam to address her, she can tell by the look on his face he saw the same thing that she did on Rufus.

"Maybe he's the killer?" Tracy said.

"Maybe," Sam repeated back.

"Welcome to the neighborhood," Tracy said, with a grin on his face.

"Do you still feel a need to talk with the neighbors Sam?"

"Only if they are engaging as our Mr. Rufus," Sam shot back. Tracy shook his head sideways. "I knew you were trouble the minute I laid eyes on you."

"I bet you did," Sam said smiling.

Tracy did not want to ask this question, but he had to. "Sam is it me or did his face appear to change?"

"No, I saw it to Tracy," Sam said. "You said that like its no big deal?" Tracy said.

"Trust me it's not when you've seen the things I have."

They were now back over to their car. "Can you be more humble?" Tracy asked. Sam looked over at Tracy, who was now leaning against the car with his hand on the roof and a worried look on his face.

"No," she said.

"Sam we are definitely going to have to talk about some things when we get back to the hotel." "I look forward to it," Sam said with a wink.

"I bet you do," Tracy replied.

Sam laughed.

As Sam now sat in the car as they cruise slowly thru the neighborhood, she now wonders if Tracy should have done his research better on her newspaper, "*The Night Turner Tribune.*" It was after all "*The Night Turner Tribune.*" A nationally syndicated paper that wasn't necessarily known for its feel-good stories and diet ads.

And this particular reporter from there didn't chase stories she chased monsters, real and imagine and whatever else went bump in the night.

Yeah, she would have that talk with him, and it would be his decision from there if he wanted to follow her into the unknown into the abyss. Because the fact was once, they went down the rabbit hole; she couldn't guarantee his safety or her own. Because, she never knew what was waiting at the bottom of that hole for her, but Sam did know one thing, *faith* in this game was like gold in *King Solomons mine* if you didn't have it you'd wish you did especially in times of peril.

Faith.

When you reach the bottom of the abyss you look back up and discovered, you now got no rope to climb back out of the darkness, but somehow you will find a way out.

Faith.

It turns out you did not need that rope, after all, to climb out of that abyss.

Sam knew what that was like, the descent into unknown and forbidden territory working in the area of paranormal investigation and reporting for her newspaper agency, *The Night Turner Tribune.*

The car was starting to feel stuffy to Sam, so she let the window down for some fresh air. The cool morning breeze blew in her face and threw her hair. She now noticed that there were more people out in the neighborhood, outside of their homes.

She wonders if Rufus had tipped some of them off about the two nosey reporters snooping around their neighborhood asking questions. She could feel some of their eyes on their vehicle as they drove past their homes. "It looks like the locals have got word about their new guest," Tracy said.

"Yeah, it looks that way," Sam replied.

Tracy looks in his rearview mirror to make sure they are not being tailed.

"What do you think about what the old man said, about the child coming back for revenge as a..." Tracy paused, unable to get the word out of his mouth.

"Demon?" Sam said.

"I guess," Tracy responded sheepishly.

"I've heard stranger things, but the only real demon to me is the one that murdered that child and is still out there roaming free," Sam affirmed.

" Speaking of that, do you know if Detective Devereaux has any solid leads on any suspects?"

"Good question, I don't know, but I got ways of finding out," Tracy said confidently. "Did I ever tell you I like the way you think," Sam said with a smile.

"All the time," Tracy said.

Sam looked back out the open window as the houses pass them by, it was good people in this neighborhood, she was sure of it, that did not deserve what had been cast upon them. Isabella family did not deserve this, no family did. She silently swore to herself that she would do everything within her power to make sure that the person that was responsible for this heinous crime would eventually be brought to justice before she left New Orleans. The killer was out there somewhere, she knew it, still lurking and waiting for his next opportunity to strike again.

If she could bring him back out from whatever rock he slither back under, like any dangerous viper, he could be cut off at the head.

"Tracy, you wouldn't happen to know the address of Isabella's parents would you?"

"In fact I do."

"I would like to pay them a visit I need to know who Isabella was?" Sam said.

"Do you think that's a good idea?" Tracy asked skeptically.

"No, I think it's a great idea," Sam said assuredly.

Tracy glanced over at Sam in the passenger seat. What was she up to now? He thought as he punched in Isabella's parents address into his car's navigation system.

His glance did not go unnoticed by Sam, and she knew somehow instinctively what he was thinking.

Yeah, she would have to have that talk with him, before they went down the rabbit hole, maybe, perhaps, together.

Chapter Six

Isabella's favorite colors were pink and blue, this Sam could see from her bedroom that had been left untouched and undisturbed from the day she had gone missing in the neighborhood, it was decorated nicely with colorful wallpaper. Isabella's favorite stuffed toys a teddy bear and a plush cat set on her bed, staring blankly into the unknown.

A few posters of her favorite boy - pop bands, adorned the non-wall paper sections of her wall.

If one were to imagine what a twelve-year-old girl's room was to look like in their mind, it would probably be this, Sam thought.

Pictures of her and family members set on various shelves in her room.

Isabella was only twelve years old at the time but looked younger than her age. She dotted on and looked up to her older brother Ben Jr. according to her parents Ben and Sharon. They were indeed good people as Sam had expected.

Just your typical working-class family that was trying to raise their children the best way that they knew how.

They had all survived *Hurricane Katrina*, and somehow they would all survive this, with the help of the Lord, the father Ben so eloquently stated to her. It did not take long for Sam to see after talking with both parents, that they held strong religious convictions and those beliefs and their faith, is still what held this family together. But there was another thing that she could not ignore as well, and that was the pain in both of their eyes as they spoke about their deceased daughter Isabella.

The only thing that Sam could assure them of is that she would do everything in her power as a reporter, to make sure that her daughter's story gets told to the public.

And although Sam could not promise them anything, in the way of finding their daughter's murderer, after all, she was not a cop.

She knew Isabella's story once published, could be a tool or the catalyst that leads to the arrest and hopefully prosecution of Isabella's killer.

Sam would make sure she would keep Isabella's story out there in the public's eye, as she silently vowed after speaking with the parents, that she would not let Isabella's death be in vain.

They thank her and Tracy for their kindness and bid them a safe trip back to the hotel.

No, Sam was not a cop.

And unknown to the killer that made her more dangerous to him, than had she been one.

• • •

The drive back to the Daupont Orleans Hotel was mostly silent, both of them deeply lost in thoughts on the morning events, expected and non-expected. It had been a rough day for both of them and what better way to unwind Sam thought than some good drinks and dinner in the Hotel's lounge. "How about you meet me back here at six o' clock for some dinner Tracy?"

"Sounds good Sam." "Also, don't forget to check into those leads for me," Sam reminded him. "I will give one of my contacts a call over at the Sex Crimes Unit and see what they got," Tracy assured Sam.

"Thanks a million, Tracy," Sam said.

Tracy could see there was something else on Sam's mind. Also, she just appeared hesitant to say what it was which he found unusual for someone that always he felt spoke their mind.

"Is there something else?" he asked.

"Come to think of it, there is, and forgive me if this second request sounds a little bizarre, but I assure you its necessary," Sam said between grinding teeth.

"What?" Tracy responded curiously.

"Do you know any good psychics?" Sam said. "What?" Tracy repeated himself. "Do you know a good psychic?" Sam said, the request flowing out of her mouth easier the second time around.

Tracy shook his head sideways in disbelief, this person he had just met over a day ago, was truly almost unbelievable, he would have to be more discreet in who he offers his liaison services to next time, he thought.

"Darling I don't have one on speed dial, but I can look into that for you," Tracy said, with a hint of condescension in his voice.

"It pays to know people," Sam said, with a smile as she exited the car. "Where have I heard that one before," Tracy said, with a roll of his eyes.

Sam laughed.

"Is there anything else you like Sam, like a *Scooby Doo Van* to go with that psychic?" Tracy asked. Sam looked at Tracy's small compact sized car.

"Well now that you asked, this little ass car is kind of crampy, a van would be roomier darling."

"Bitch," Tracy said under his breath.

"Likewise," Sam said as she gave him a smile and a wink.

"Three o' clock," she said. Tracy laughed, he had to admit to himself, he liked her. He only wished he knew where she was going with this ghoul hunting shit, as he pulled out of the hotel's parking lot.

He shifted in the rental car seat to get more comfortable; she was right a van would be nicer. He'll check into that later. After that is, he finds her a psychic. Which shouldn't be that hard to do, he reckons in a city entrenched in what some would consider unorthodox practices of religion, like New Orleans voodoo. But to other people that lived here, it was a part of everyday life, like a good bowl of Creole Gumbo, what you put in it, more than often determine what you got out of it in flavor and taste.

Tracy now wondered if he had gotten himself into something that was above his pay-grade. He had important questions that nagged at his subconscious, like who was Samantha Jackson? And what was she doing here? He would have to do some digging and some soul searching at the same time, he thought.

Nevertheless, though, he could not deny the fact that there was a child-killer still on the loose, and if he could be instrumental in catching the sonofabitch, he was all hands on deck.

Because maybe that was a risk he might have to take, to make the streets of New Orleans safer, from this particular type of monster.

But first he had a psychic to look up, what the hell did Sam have up her sleeve? He thought as he pulled into the driveway of his house.

Psychics? What next Ufo's he thought, hold up, I better not put that out there in the universe, he thought to himself.

"Things were already weird enough, and it'll be just my luck if things got weirder," he mumbled to himself as he exited his car.

As he made his way to his front door, he just so happen to glance up at the sky just for reassurances nervously.

Chapter Seven

"Hey babe, how's it going down there in New Orleans?" the cheerful voice said on the other end of the phone. "Great baby," Sam said to Brandon. It was good to hear his voice. "I miss you," he said sweetly. "I miss you too," she reciprocated.

"How's the weather down there?" "Cool, but lovely," Sam said. "I wish I were there Sam." "Awww, me too," Sam cooed, empathetically. "Do you have any idea when you'll be back?" "Hopefully by next week baby, but you know how these assignments go," Sam said.

"Yeah, I know, that's what I get for dating a big-time investigative reporter," Brandon quip.

"Reporter, yes, big-time I don't know about that?" Sam said, with a laugh.

"That's what I love about you Sam you're so humble about your awesomeness," Brandon said.

"Hey if you're trying to talk your way up to some phone sex, it's not happening today," Sam said, with a smile on her face.

Brandon laughed. "Guilty as charged," he said. "Okay baby I just got dispatch for a run, I'll give you a call later on tonight," Brandon said with a sudden urgency in his voice. "Okay, baby be safe." "I will."

Sam, could hear the dispatcher voice on Brandon's patrol car radio in the background giving out the information on his run, for some reason this always made her feel slightly uncomfortable.

'I love you," she said. "I love you too," Brandon reciprocated. "Awww ain't that sweetttt." Sam heard another familiar male voice in the background say. "Who's that Ty? Tell him I said Hi," Sam said with a laugh. "Sam said Hi Jerk," Brandon said to his patrol and squad car partner, Tyrone Johnson. "Hi, Sam," she heard Ty shout out to her in the background. "Okay, babe I gotta go."

"Okay, baby, be safe," Sam repeated herself. "You too," Brandon said.

Sam ended the call on her cell phone; she had always made it a point, especially since Brandon, had started his job with the Chicago Police Department as a police officer, to tell him that she loved him, even if they had a disagreement or lover's quarrel earlier.

She knew how dangerous his job was and if something was ever to happen to him out on the tough streets of Chicago, she could not fathom him remembering, that the last time that they spoke with each other, it was of anger and not love.

Sam knew this was a selfish and unrealistic expectation of herself and him, but it was better than the latter, and that's all that matter to her right now. All she could do is hope that her request to him (To be safe) did not go unheeded and that he would return home safely. In retrospect though, she was sure he felt the same way about her.

"Enough of being a worry wart," Sam thought, as she sat the cell phone down on top of her hotel dresser. She knew worrying did no one any good, not even the worrier; it was she felt, a reaction that in fact produce inactive solutions if not viewed from a logical perspective of the dynamics of the issue, personal or non-personal.

Bottom line was Brandon could handle himself and so could she. And right now she knew she had more pressing matters at hand like a six 'o clock dinner date with her liaison Tracy Leaumont. Sam poured what was left over of the *Pinot noir* in a wine glass, and headed off to her hotel's bathroom for a hot shower and to get ready for what she was sure was going to be anything but an unremarkable evening, rest assured she would not be disappointed.

It had not been easy for Tracy to locate a reputable psychic that one of his contacts could vouch for but finally, after numerous attempts, he had come by one that a longtime friend and associate had sworn by, a psychic that went by the name of Madame Ashante Delacroix.

After contacting her and after much negotiation and assuring her that he would make it worth her time she had agreed to meet with him and Sam tomorrow at the crime scene, to discuss the case of the most recent homicides in the lower ninth ward. When he questioned her about why she had proposed to meet them there, instead of at another location, she went into a spill about that she had to be there on-site where the murders had taken place to get the best results thru her clairvoyant abilities. It sounded weird enough to be believable, so he reluctantly accepted her terms.

The truth of the matter was though, that old dilapidated house gave him a bad vibe one that he felt even a good hot shower couldn't wash off. But he could not deny either that he was curious to see if this Madame Ashante was the real deal. Tracy looked at his wristwatch; he was fifteen minutes early as he pulled into valet parking at the Daupont Orleans Hotel.

Chapter Eight

The tattered blueish gray cat made its way stealthily down the street of a row of abandon homes in the eighth ward. It went about its business unnoticed like the dilapidated homes that set on this street.

The cat was cold and thirsty from its journey and had not eaten or drink anything in a week. The cool water puddle from the rain that had recently fallen was a welcome watery banquet as it lapped up gulps of it with its tongue. Its five senses of feline perception were on full alert as its bright green eyes took in its new surroundings. It massaged the side of its body up against a broken mailbox post purring in delight.

But that only brought her temporary satisfaction; her mind told her that she was close to him, she was home. The tattered cat jotted off into one of the abandon homes to find her something delectable to eat to sustain herself for the task she came all this way to complete. She was looking for a particular rat to catch, one that had evaded her in the past. She could smell his stench nearby, sense his presence, he was crafty and good at going undetected, but so was she. Oh' he wasn't the kind of rat you could lure with a piece of cheese, he had other things in mind, other things on his agenda.

Oh' but so did she and that's how she would catch him, that's how she would ensnare him. And when she finally had him in her claws, his beady little black eyes will look again into her bright green ones and realize playtime's over - endgame.

The smell of decomposing fish wrapped up in a newspaper caught a whiff of her nostrils; She walked over there slowly to it and cautiously to inspect her find.

Did someone know she would be here, did someone know she would come?

Meowww.

She begins to feast, on the pungent fish. Her belly will be full tonight.

And then she will find a corner or some hidden place in the abandoned house and cuddle up and sleep until night comes.

The cat stopped eating and raised her head again sniffing the air, her pupils widening, the hairs raised on her back.

The smell of the rat nearby was almost as pungent as the fish she was eating.

Maybe he was miles away, she thought, maybe he was close? Not that it matters she reasoned, the outcome would be the same.

Meowww, - death.

Chapter Nine

He was an unassuming individual, someone that you would pass by on the street and never notice. And frankly, he liked it that way. A man of measurable girth, with greasy hair and a five o clock shadow of stubble on his face, he had eyes that appeared to look straight thru you when he was talking to you.

His name was Moby, and he was a janitor by trade at the local High School nearby in the ninth ward, he was married and had a sixteen-year-old stepdaughter of his own that he despised with a passion because the wife dotted on the little brat like she was the second coming or something he thought. To him, all she was he thought was a selfish little bitch that got way more than she deserved from her mother and him.

Things had been fine he thought between her mother and him until she came back onto the scene to live with them at fourteen years of age because she wasn't getting along with her biological dad.

Moby now felt that his marital bliss had suddenly turned into three years of living hell. In a way, he felt envy and empathy for her biological father being able to tolerate her so long and envy for finally being rid of the brat.

(Secrets).

Moby had them big and small. Secrets that he kept hidden from her and his wife. Big ones like he had served time in one of California's State Prison, for Rape and Assault with Attempt to Commit Murder. He had cope a plea and got twenty but only did ten and got paroled out early on good behavior if there was such a thing for a man like him.

He had moved around a lot after getting paroled from prison but found obtaining a job and keeping one as a registered sex offender was a very hard thing to do, once his employer discovered what he had served time for in the joint. Even harder was finding a community that he could live in that would not ostracize him and ban together to throw his ass out once they discovered who he was.

Meanwhile, he was still fighting his urges, his desires to repeat the behavior that had gotten him that ten years of lockdown in the first place.

Until one day he just said to himself, "Fuck em' all." The probation officer, the registering, the world.

He moved away from it all, and never looked back. He got himself a new identity, and most of all a new start when he touched down in New Orleans. He tried to keep his urges at bay, but the monster inside of him would not allow it.

Moby felt he had been screwed over, for the most part, all his life by the women in his life, especially his birth mom who he thought was his sister up until the age of twenty-five. His grandparents had raised him under the pretense that they were his parent's until; he had discovered the lie.

Moby believed he could have been anything in life if not for the bad breaks due to other people's misconceptions about him. Instead, here he was reduced to the lowly status of a custodial janitor in a public high school cleaning out the Urinals and Shit Stalls of thankless, and ungrateful acne prone pus-popping teenagers who to him was much like his unappreciative stepdaughter.

If he were not married to her mom, he would have - wait he thought.

Was this not the same kind of thinking that had gotten him into trouble before? What his prison psychiatrist had warned him of in his sessions.

His mind wandered back to the little girl; he did not mean to kill her; he had lost control given in to the monster inside of him, he thought.

He was a sick man, but his twisted thoughts and desires would not allow him to admit that he was. But somewhere in the deep recesses of his mind, Moby knew one day he would have to answer to someone, something, for the things that he has done.

What he didn't know was that day was coming sooner then he had anticipated.

Meowww.

A grayish blue cat observed him with bright green eyes from the distance of an open doorway as he put the janitorial supplies up he had been using in a nearby supply closet.

A strange feeling came over Moby as he quickly turned around to see what was behind him.

He watched as the cat quickly darted off out of the open doorway.

"Stupid cat," he mumbled.

The school bell ringed, and the students begin exiting their classes, exiting the school building for the day.

Moby watched them keenly as they left.

Know - nothing's, he thought, as he went back to putting up the janitorial supplies before he also left for the day.

The cat reappeared in the doorway and watched him quietly; one could say almost sizing him up, biding its time.

The sweet smell of revenge hung in the air, and unfortunately for Moby, the little creature that was now stalking him was the only one that could smell its intoxicating fragrance.

The cat noted that the man that now stood before her again had not change that much at all after its death. He was still as disgusting as ever, a vile pig in human form that took whatever he wanted even the innocence of lambs.

She also knew now in her infinite wisdom that there was no rehabilitating these types that had crossed the point of no return.

What had he told her thru foul his smelling breath that reaped of stale cigarettes? As his massive body weight down on her, almost crushing her small frame. "She was not the first and won't be the last."

Moby was what he was behind the mask that he wore.

A monster.

Isabella knew that. But Izzy knew it better!

Chapter Ten

The Daupont lounge inside of the hotel was just as cozy and quaint as the hotel itself. As Tracy spotted Sam sitting at one of its many dining room tables, he made his way over to join her, while graciously declining the assistance of the host at the front entrance who greeted him.

"Good evening," Tracy said as he joins Sam at the dining table where she was sitting. "Evening," Sam replied with a smile. A young waiter soon approached their table and offered them drinks and a menu.

"Two glasses of water and a bottle of Lambrusco," Sam requested. "Coming up," the waiter said politely.

Their waiter soon returns shortly with glasses of waters and a bottle of red wine; he pours the wine into two additional empty wine glasses he has brought along with the water. Sam and Tracy thanks him and he agrees, to return shortly to take their dinner order.

Sam takes a sip of the water first as she looks across at Tracy dressed in a casual blue blazer with a crisp white shirt. "I must say you are looking mighty dapper tonight."

"Thanks, you're looking pretty good yourself Sam, that white dress becomes you," Tracy responds.

"Thanks, it's just something I pulled out of my suitcase," Sam said trying to be modest. Tracy smiled at her reply.

Sam could almost feel the heat of Tracy's eye's go over her again, and despite his male - model looks, she had to admit it made her slightly uncomfortable or was it she wondered due to the latter.

"You should pull it out more often," Tracy said with that glint in his eye.

Now that took Sam off guard, was Tracy hitting on her? She now wondered, or just testing the waters.

"I think we need a toast," Sam proposed, as she lifted up her glass of red wine. "Too what?" Tracy asked.

"To friendship," Sam stated.

"There" she had strategically placed Tracy in the friend zone, she thought, as their wine glasses clanged together.

"Friends huh?" Tracy said, eyeing Sam suspiciously. "I hope so," Sam rebuttal.

"Friends like girlfriends?" Tracy asked.

"No, friends like friends," Sam said, now wondering if her objective had backfired.

"You mean like professional friends?" Tracy persisted.

"I mean like I don't need this shit you're giving me right now Tracy," Sam shouted out angrily. Drawing unwanted attention and eyes from other patrons toward their table.

Sam noticed that Tracy looked slightly shocked by her reaction, maybe she had gone a little overboard she thought.

All of a sudden to Sam's dismay Tracy started laughing. "What the hell is so funny?" Sam said still pissed.

"The look on your face Sam, I was just fucking with you," he said.

"You was just what?" Sam said, not amused.

"Look you're cute and all, but you're not my type darling," he said.

"The feeling is mutual you pompous asshole," Sam said, as she took another sip of her wine.

Wait she thought, why was she hurt by his admission, wasn't she the one that just put him in the friend zone? And wait, did he "just" refer to her as darling? She was such a presumptuous fool she thought.

She could not help but laugh at herself, Tracy was right she wasn't his type.

"I hope this means that our, dinner date didn't go to hell in a handbasket because of my uncanny sense of humor?" Tracy said, almost apologetic.

Sam smiled, "Your uncanny sense of humor, now that I can toast to," she said.

Tracy smiled and raised his glass." A mental note, I do not unnecessarily get on this bitch wrong side" Tracy thought to himself.

"By the way what is your type?" Sam asked Tracy not willing to let him off the hook so easily.

Sam looked back over at the host that greeted him at the door; Sam followed his eyes.

"I think the host is kinda' cute wouldn't you agree?" he said.

"Nope not my type either," Sam said.

"Bitch!" Tracy said and laughed.

"The feelings mutual," Sam said, raising her glass in the air.

The waiter came back over to the table, and the both of them ordered a light entrée off the menu for dinner with a house salad.

"Now that we have established your sexual preference which was none of my damn business in the first place, can we get down to the business at hand?"

Tracy could do nothing but smile from within at that remark, that was one of the things that he liked about Sam, unlike some people that were just pretentious assholes that would think one thing while their mouth was saying another, he did not get this impression from his new friend.

If she thought about it, you could guarantee that she would more then often say it, good or bad.

"Fair enough, where do you want me to start?" Tracy asked as he played thru the salad in the bowl that was now in front of him.

"Wherever you want?" Sam said.

Tracy smiled, for whatever reason, the atmosphere now felt more relaxed between him and the reporter.

"Well I did contact my contacts over at Sex Crimes and Homicide, but they did not have anyone that they had narrowed down as a prime suspect in the murder of that little girl."

"That's too bad," Sam said disappointedly.

"Yes, it is," Tracy agreed.

"Now for the good news, or not. I was able to secure you that psychic you asked for Sam."

"I like the way you put that, who is it?"

"Madame Ashante Delacroix ." Oooh - I like her already," Sam said.

"I figure you would," Tracy concurred.

"So when do I meet this Madame Ashante?" Sam asked.

"Hopefully tomorrow, she has agreed to meet us at the house in the lower ninth ward," Tracy said reluctantly.

"I think I know why Tracy, there is so much negative energy in that house; you can cut it with a knife."

"I think an ax would be more like it," Tracy proposed.

"Thank you," Sam said, as the waiter now set her and Tracy 's entrees on the table. The smell of good hot food now feels both of their nostrils.

Sam had detected that sense of reservation in Tracy's voice about going back to the house to the crime scene. And although he had said he would be going, she did not feel it would be fair to him if she did not address that matter. See to her it all boil down again to rather are not Tracy was on his "own admission" willing to follow her voluntarily down that rabbit hole.

"Tracy you know, I appreciate all your assistance with this case, but I must let you know that it may get very dangerous from here, and if you don't want to continue this investigation with me I understand."

Tracy took in every word that Sam had just said, as he rubbed the sides of his chin with his hand. Here was his chance he thought to bow out or bow in on an investigation that he had acknowledged was above his pay - grade.

He was a lot of things, he thought, but one of them for sure was not a coward.

"Why would I do that you selfish bitch and let you have all the fun?" he said sarcastically.

"Yeah, why would you?" Sam said with a smile and a wink.

Chapter Eleven

Moby knew he had no business going back to that location again, where he had allowed the monster inside of him make bad things happen again. But something was calling him back, something he could not resist.

That something now kept him awake constantly at night. A desire that was haunting him in what little shut-eye he was able to obtain when he did finally drift off to sleep. It wasn't like he had ever been a man of conscious or empathy towards other people feelings. No! A conscious always play second fiddle or maybe even third to Moby's sociopathic and narcissistic twisted desires.

Desire, yes that is what he was feeling, overwhelming in its essence in its depravity to draw him back to the place where he had left little Isabella's lifeless body, lying on the floor in that old dilapidated house in the lower ninth ward. If he did not know any better himself, he would have thought it was the dead girl's spirit itself drawing him back into the tentacles of that place that he vowed never to return to again. But then he knew better than that, didn't he? She had not been his first victim and the way Moby felt right now if he couldn't control that monster inside of him that always wanted to get out and she surely would not be his last.

And although Moby had bull-shitted and finagled the prison parole board into granting him an early release on the pretense that he was the new-and-improved 3.0 Moby, rehabilitated, he knew all along that he never had any plan or intentions of meeting those obligations now or ever. In fact, if he had been honest with the State of California's parole board and told them the truth.

The truth that all he ever thought about while being locked up was getting out and getting his head back into the game, as he looked over and studied page after page of young women on the illegal contraband (Teen magazines) inside his cell that he was not supposed to have due to his conviction. They would have thrown away his jail key and politely told him to go fuck himself.

He had vowed never to return because Moby knew men like him weren't the most popular amongst other inmates. In fact, Men like him in prison that preyed on the innocent that preyed on children in the real world. (The outside) was like shit scum on a inmates boot.

That is when the killing started after he had made that vow, which he would never return to prison again. He also made another one that he would never leave another witness alive again. Dark promises to himself that he had made good on so far.

No more time for contemplation, who was Moby kidding he thought? The Monster inside of him demanded to be fed. He would return to the lower ninth ward today and use the same cloak of invisibility that had shielded him from detection the last time.

A vehicle that he stored away and only drove on what he called special occasions, a car that Moby had outfitted with all the bells and whistles to look very similar to an unmarked patrol car.

When he drove that car, he was no longer Moby, the janitor. He assumed a new identity, Investigator Mike Fox, just another cop passing thru a neighborhood to the untrained eye, except he wasn't a cop, he was an impersonator and at worst a killer.

Moby raised the garage door up as he looked over his fake police car a black 1989 Ford Crown Victoria Police Interceptor. The Car at one time had been part of New Orleans Police Department's Fleet, but had been decommissioned, and stripped of its police insignia and equipment and sold at a public auction.

That's where Moby step in and restore it back to almost its original status, including a brand new police scanner so that he could monitor and track police calls.

What better way he thought to slap the cops in their faces and say I am smarter than you "assholes," was to drive around in a vehicle like theirs while he was out committing his atrocities.

Moby smile as he entered the Crown Victoria and put the key in the ignition. He gave the ignition switch a turn and the car rumble to life. He hit the gas pedal, and the car gave an even more throaty rumble from its 4.6-liter Modular V8 engine.

The car with its fake officialness, made him feel like he was powerful and indestructible.

"What the hell, one last time," Moby said to himself as he pulled out of his driveway, headed to the other side of town, back to the lower ninth ward.

"Unaware" that's exactly what it would be, one last trip.

Chapter Twelve

Moby had made it a point despite his fake cover, to return to his crime scene very early in the morning before dawn, to avoid drawing any unwanted attention to himself. He was not sure if the police still had the house under surveillance or not, so he parked his fake police car on the opposite side of the street further down from the house to get a feel for his surroundings first. Moby opened up his glove compartment to his car and pulled out the small pair of binoculars he kept inside of it.

He flips them open and puts them to his eyes, adjusting the optics on them so that he can zoom in and get a better look at the house and its surrounding area. No cops, he thinks, as he shuts the collapsible binoculars and stuffs them back into his glove compartment.

That feeling comes over him again as he sits there in his car staring off in the direction of the house. Bam! Something hits his window on the driver side jarring him out of his trance-like focus. Bam! Again. A closed fist slams up against his tinted window.

"Goddammit!" Moby says as he hits his window switch, slowly letting it down but not all the way. A pair of wild eyes stares back at him thru the crack of the window. "What the fuck is your problem buddy?" Moby asks in the most official police voice that he can muster up.

"Have yall caught that girls killer yet?" the eyes answer back.

Moby can smell the strong odor of alcohol coming from his new inquisitive friend thru the window.

"Not yet we are working on it," in his police voice.

"Well work harder!" his new friend shouts back at him thru stale breath and red eyes.

Moby lowers his window some more to get a better look at the stranger.

The man looks to him like a hobo living off the streets.

Moby watches him as he takes a bottle out of his coat pocket and turns it up to his lips taking big gulps of whatever the elixir is in his glass container.

"Its kind of early in the day for that wouldn't you agree?" Moby said.

"No, I would not!" the stranger answer back defiantly, wiping his mouth off with his sleeve.

"It's never too early in the day for refreshments," he added.

The stranger's eyes suddenly widen as he gets a better look inside the car, a better look at Moby.

"Don't I know you?" he asks Moby, trying to place his face thru a mental fog.

"I don't think so," Moby said affirmatively.

His new friend was now starting to annoy him, and he knew that could be detrimental to them both. Moby reason it would take him two seconds maybe three to cut the bum's throat. He could envision the blood pouring out of the strangers gaping wound onto the seat of his car. He smiled at the thought.

Stick to the plan his voice told him in his head.

One,

Two,

The vagrant stared at him some more. "I guess not," he said.

Moby slid the switchblade knife back between the front seat of his car.

"You guessed right," Moby replied with a solemn look on his face, almost one of disappointment.

Rufus grumbled something incoherently and walked away from the fake police car, away from Moby in the opposite direction of the house.

Moby watched him closely thru slitted pig eyes that almost didn't appear human.

When Rufus had disappeared and was no longer within his eyesight, Moby turned his attention back over to the house; and that is when he spotted her, a young girl that bore a striking resemblance to the one that he had murdered. She now stood no more than twenty-five yards away from the house staring in his direction.

"What the fuck?" Moby muttered underneath his breath, as his brain still tried to register what he was seeing. Was it an apparition, was she even real? He thought. The young girl gesture with her hand for him to follow her as she turned around and began walking towards the direction of the house. Moby watched her too thru those same slitted pig eyes of his as he exited his fake police car.

He looked around to see if anyone was following her if the hobo was still around. The street was eerily quiet. It appeared to him that no one else was around. What the hell was a young girl like her doing out at this time of the hour? He thought. Was this a set-up? Is this why he had been compelled to come back to this location? He reached back into his car and pulled out the switchblade knife wedged between his car seat and stuffed it inside his jacket pocket. He then walked around to the back of his car, popped the trunk, reached in and pulled out a black bag that he had aptly name his kill kit. Moby looked back around and shut the trunk to his fake police car. He did not yet have any of the answers to the questions that he needed, but one thing for sure, he did have the audacity no matter how foolish to go and seek those answers out.

And that's just what Izzy had banked on.

Moby caught another glimpse of the girl entering the dilapidated house.

It had appeared that she had turned around and looked back at him again, but he wasn't for sure. "You wanna play games you little bitch, will play," he murmured with a sinister tone in his voice.

Moby then made his way as fast as his fat frame could carry him across the street with the kill bag in hand to the house the girl had just entered.

Someone watched him quietly and undetected from a distance.

• • •

Tracy watched as Sam exited the Daupoint Hotel with a camera around her neck and two cups in her hand. "Nice Scooby Van," she said as Tracy open the door for her and she entered the vehicle. "I thought you'd like the new wheels," Tracy said confidently. "I do," Sam reciprocated. "How did you sleep last night?" Sam ask Tracy.

"Not much," he said. "And you?"

"Like a baby," Sam said with a smile. "It figures," he said, shaking his head. "Awwww, don't be a sourpuss," Sam said as she leaned over and pinched Tracy's cheek. "Look I brought you coffee," she said pointing to the two cups that she had placed in the front cup holder.

Tracy picked up one of the cups of coffee and took a sip. " Mmmm that's delicious that's not just coffee that's a *vanilla mocha latte*, honey you're redeemed."

"Thanks, and for the record, I did not sleep much either," Sam confessed.

"I knew that," Tracy said with a smirk on his face, as he took another sip of his coffee.

"This Madame Ashante Delacroix, why didn't she just ride with us Trace?" Sam asked, out curiosity.

"I offered, she declined," Tracy said.

"Why?"

"Something about not wanting her energy broken," Tracy answered.

"Bitch," Sam said. "That's the same thing I thought," Tracy stated.

"Why does that not surprise me, Tracy."

They both laughed.

It felt good to Sam that she and Tracy could share this brief period of levity together, helped relieved some of the stress she was sure they both felt working a case like this, that was so intense and demanding.

"Hopefully," she thought this Madame Ashante would offer them some insight into the investigation, if not just a glimmer of information, that might be instrumental in apprehending this animal that was still at large.

She need not worry about that though. Her and Tracy would get their money's worth and then some. Because Madame Ashante Delacroix wasn't a poser, she was the real deal which they would soon find out.

Sam looked across at Tracy; he appeared tense.

They were now only twenty minutes away from the lower ninth ward, twenty minutes away from the house.

Chapter Thirteen

Moby cautiously entered the house; he had not planned on returning so soon to these killing grounds, he thought. But he had unfinished business, and today he would not leave until that business was finish.

The girl had entered this house; this he was for sure, it was now his job to find her, and once he found her he would make her regret that she called him back here to play. Memories of what he had done here and the innocent blood he had shed flooded his senses, as the familiar stench of the house flooded his nostrils. His eyes darted back and forth across the inside of the house, trying to adjust to its dusty darkness.

Heeheehee - comes the sound of a young girl giggling out of nowhere, stopping Moby in his tracks, raising the hairs on his arms.

A shadow of something quickly shoots pass him, causing him to spin around with the switchblade in his hand. He quickly ejects the blade, but is too slow and does not see what runs pass him.

Heeheehee, more giggling. His senses are on full alert now, as his eyes scan the room. Moby feels something tap him on the back of the neck. He turns around and swiftly stabs the naked air, nothing is there.

Whatever it was is now gone. "What the fuck is going on?" He says in a whisper of a voice to himself.

"Man you are losing it, keep your shit together," he assures himself.

His eyes catch the writing on the wall; he walks over to it to get a closer look. And although the wall is bleeding the words in crimson red, bleeding the words in blood, he can still make out what it said. ***"Beware of Izzy."***

Moby reaches out and touches the words on the wall. "Shit!" he screams out as he quickly draws his hand back in searing pain, but it's too late, his fingers now have first degree burns and quickly starts to blister.

Touching the foreboding words of blood on the wall is like touching acid.

"I am going to enjoy this you fucking little bitch!" he screams out.

"Hehehehe, you can't catch me," she says as she darts up the stairs.

Moby catches a glimpse of a figure in a pink dress running up the stairway; he runs after her. "I got you now you little… aaargh!" Moby screams out in pain as a nine-inch nail protruding thru one of the steps goes thru his shoe into his foot penetrating soft flesh. He loses his balance and doubles back, his fat frame falling down the rest of the stairway to the bottom of the landing, his bag still in his hand.

Hehehehe, the laughter tauntings him. "I think you broke my fucking back you little bastard," he says writhing in pain as he attempts to recover from the fall. He throws the kill bag down on the floor away from him. He then watches in awe as the bag moves slowly across the floor away from him as if guided by some unforeseen force, it then picks up momentum and is dragged across the floor by the same unforeseen force into one of the numerous rooms in the house, as it disappears from his line of sight.

"How did you do that he?" He stammers.

"It doesn't matter, I still have this," he says brandishing his switchblade knife, waving it in the air.

"And I am coming for you," he says attempting to hide the fear that is now starting to set in on his mind. His attention goes back down to his foot.

He makes a quick mental assessment of his injuries, burned hand, his whole body aches, from the fall, now a nail implanted in his foot, it wasn't supposed to be this hard he thinks, for God sakes, she is only a twelve-year-old girl or is she?

"All I need to do is get this fucking nail out my foot, and your ass is mine," he warns as he reaches down thru clenched teeth and begins pulling the hot nail out of his foot tearing the flesh off his stubby fingers in the process.

"Fuckkkk!" he screams out as the nail finally comes out.

He tosses the bloody nail to the floor.

"Hehehehe, come and get me," he hears a little girl voice say, which sounds like its coming from one of the upstairs room.

But something in his mind starts to tell him this is no little girl; maybe he should leave he thinks, as he gets back on his feet. Sweat now rolls down his fleshy face; his slitted pig eyes are even more narrow as he tries to focus on his surroundings. Maybe he should try a different approach he reasons.

"Do you want to play with Izzy?" he hears the little girl voice say.

Moby looks up the stairs; he hesitates at first to move in that direction, what if it's a trap? He thinks. Fuck it! She's just a little girl he reasons, what the hell is wrong with him? "Get a grip!" he tells himself.

Moby proceeds now more cautiously up the stairway, watching his every step, listening for every sound.

When he reaches the top landing safely, he lets out a sigh of relief. "Now back to business," he tells himself.

This little *Home alone bitch* is not going to get the best of him, he reasons.

There are two more rooms on the upper floor.

Contestant, door number one, or door number two?

An imaginary game show host asks him in his mind.

The game show host smiles showing unnaturally white teeth, but his eyes are what stand out the most they have no color in them both are completely bloodshot red.

Contestant, door number one or door number two?

Roby attempts to shake the image from his head. "Fuck You!" he says out loud to no one in particular.

That is when he catches something out the side of his eye running pass him from one of the rooms, he spins around and grabs a handful of her hair from the back of her head.

"I gotcha now you little bitch!" he says gleefully, as he turns the little girl around to face him.

His face goes blank as his jaw drops in horror! Because what he is now staring at could hardly be misconstrued as a human-less alone a little girl. It's skull-like face stares back at him thru hollow eye sockets, it then slowly smiles at him revealing a double row of rotten razor-like teeth in its mouth.

Razorlike teeth that before he knows it clamps down on his hand. "Goddammit!" he screams out as he releases the thing's hair.

Once released, it quickly wastes no time and maneuvers to his side in a blink of an eye, it grabs the switchblade knife out his hand and plunges the knife up into his scrotum. Moby eyes go wide as an intense sense of excruciating pain hits his brain, pain that locks his throat into a silent scream.

Blood instantly starts gushing out of his testicles running down his pants leg. The knife protrudes downward like a phallus between his legs.

"Hehehehe, do you want to play some more with Izzy, Moby?" it asks him in its little girl voice.

Moby is now trembling with fear the same fear that he instilled in his helpless victims.

"Do youuuu!" it shouts at him in a more masculine voice.

"What the fuck are you?" Moby asks as he crouches over in pain, backing away from the thing towards the stairs. He feels himself now starting to get dizzy; he knows he is losing to much blood, and it is just a matter of time before he goes into shock.

"Isabella," says the thing that is no longer the hideous creature that was standing before him, it is the little girl that he has murdered.

Moby begins to sob and begins pleading for his life. "I didn't mean to kill you, child. I am not a bad man."

Isabella leans her head inquisitively to the side. "You are not?"

"No, I am not. Sometimes, I can't help myself, and the *monster* inside of me makes me do bad things," Moby said, coughing up blood.

Isabella stood there, now silent.

The knife to Moby felt as if it was tearing his insides up, it had to come out. He blocks out the pain and reaches between his legs and pulls the knife out with one jerk! He almost passes out.

"I have a present for you," he says with a grin, as he holds the knife towards Isabella.

"I have one for you too," she says calmly.

"What?"

Her face changes back into the skull mask.

"Death," she answers.

"Fuck you!" Moby says defiantly, as he begins making his way towards Isabella, wielding his knife in one hand.

Meowww, a black cat lunges at Moby out of nowhere and is on his face with its claws in his eyes before he takes another step towards Isabella.

Moby let out a shriek of pain as he fights with the little black beast that was now on his face, clawing and tearing!

"Get the fuck off me!" he yells as he backs up blindly to the upper edge of the stairway.

He manages to rip the cat off his face but loses his balance and falls back down the flight of stairs, one of his legs snaps on impact before he finally lands at the bottom of the stairs on the floor.

Moby lays there for a moment before he finally comes too.

Meowww, the cat watches him unhurt at the top of the stairway.

One of his legs is now a bent and broken mess, as he attempts to crawl towards the front door towards freedom.

"Help me! He shouts out. Please somebody help meee!"

Hehehehe.

"Don't you want to play?"

Chapter Fourteen

Tracy pulled the van up behind an orange compact sized Volkswagen with a soft black top, parked in front of the condemned house. "That must be her," Sam presumed. "Must be," Tracy echoed, as they both proceeded to exit the van. The sound of the van doors closing broke the silence in the morning air.

Madame Ashante exited her vehicle, upon seeing Sam and Tracy pull up behind her. She was an attractive woman of medium build, with a honey brown complexion and braided hair. She wore a colorful dashiki dress with various protective amulets and beads.

"Good Morning Madame Ashante," Sam said as she greeted her. "Good Morning you must be Samantha?" Ashante said as she shook Sam's hand.

"And you must be the gentleman I spoke with on the phone?" Ashante said as she turns in Tracy's direction. "That's correct, Tracy Beaumont in the flesh," he said with a smile, as he shook her hand.

"Glad to make both of your acquaintances, how can I be of help?"

"As I discussed with you on the phone Madame Ashante this is the house where that little girl was murdered. If you can come inside and get a feel of the place, any information you can provide us with now or later would be greatly appreciated," Tracy said.

Ashante looked over at the house.

"I don't know why for the life of me they leave places like this still standing?" she said with a sense of disgust.

"It's not only a blight on the neighborhood. It's a blight on the soul," she added.

"I could not agree with you more," Tracy said.

"Just standing here in front of this house, I can feel the negative energy surging thru it," Ashante observed.

"Well let's see what secrets she has" Ashante proposed.

"Sounds good to me," Sam interjected.

The three of them proceeded towards the front porch.

"I would not go in there if I was you!" A voice commanded, stopping them in their tracks.

All three of them turned around to face the voice it was old man Rufus.

"Rufus we don't have any time for your nonsense today," Tracy said.

"Nonsense you say? You have no idea what you are dealing with Mr. Beaumont!"

Madame Ashante instantly felt a psychic connection with Rufus as her eyes rolled back in her head only revealing the whites of them she starts convulsing, as she stretches out her hands towards him.

"Madame Ashante are you okay?" Tracy asks concerned.

Sam quickly intervene. "Don't touch her Tracy! She's okay; she is in a trance right now," Sam said as she pushed Tracy aside.

"Look," Sam said as she pointed to Rufus.

Tracy looked on in amazement, Rufus eyes too were a ghastly white also, and without color and he was shaking uncontrollably as well while still standing on his feet.

Madame Ashante Delacroix could see it all as the visions of what had happened flooded her head. The sadistic killer is assaulting the young girl, leaving her on the floor to die. Leaving her in the filthy confines of the decrepit and condemned house to die alone.

Wait! She wasn't alone when she died. Madame Ashante could see now that someone had come along right before Isabella took her last breaths here on earth and performed a ritual on her to come back and seek out her murderer before her soul was at rest.

That someone, was a Shaman, and that someone, was no one other than Rufus.

Madame Ashante snapped out of her trance, and her eyes returned to normal at the same time Rufus appeared to simultaneously snap out of whatever held him in a hypnotic state as well.

"What did you do to her? she asked him firmly.

Sam and Tracy looked on in confusion.

"I did not… not kill her!" he stammer.

"I only gave her the ability to return from beyond to make things right," Rufus insisted.

"To make things right," he repeated softly this time.

"Revenge," Madame Ashante said.

"What's going on?" Sam said.

"Rufus, here is a Shaman, he came upon the girl after the killer had left and performed a ritual on her to bring back a spirit that would seek out revenge for the girl's death," Ashante said.

"That is some heavy shit," Tracy said, wide-eyed.

He looked over at Rufus who had his head down. "Next time can you just dial 911."

A scream interrupted them coming from the house.

"Helpppp me!" the voice screamed out in agony.

The door to the house this time seemed like it took forever to breach, as Tracy rammed his shoulder into it several times before it finally burst open.

The three of them entered the house slowly, only to see the shocking sight of the bloody figure, "Moby" crawling towards them while pleading for there help.

"My God," Tracy whispers.

"God has nothing to do with this," Ashante says.

The whole room suddenly feels as if it's vibrating as the three of them watch as a fault line begins to form in the ceiling, as it begins to crack, they all try to keep their balance as the house shakes and rumbles as if seized by an earthquake.

The heavy metal chandelier swings from the ceiling above and begins to loosen from its foundation as plaster falls from the ceiling like rain.

"Helpppp!" Moby screams out again.

Tracy attempts to make his way towards Moby when Sam tackles him to the floor. A split second before the heavy metal chandelier disengages itself from the ceiling and plummets down on Moby's head causing it to burst open like a bloody melon.

The house stops shaking and is now silent.

"Fuck!" Tracy blurts out as he looks on in disbelief at the unknown man underneath the chandelier.

"Who is he?" Tracy asks.

Sam slowly walks over to the black bag that's open on the floor she looks inside of it and sees duct tape, rope, and various tools of torture.

"I suspect the killer," she says solemnly.

Hehehehehe, giggling in the distance of the house. "Did you hear that?" Sam says.

"Yes, I heard it, and I don't like it," Tracy responded.

The three of them followed the voice of the little girl to an apparition of her dressed in a pink and blue dress standing at the top of the stairway.

Madame Ashante walked slowly over to the stairway.

"Izzy."

"Yes," she answered.

"Its okay baby, don't be afraid, go to the light," Ashante said.

"The light."

'Yes, go home," Ashante insisted.

"The light is beautiful," Izzy said.

"Yes, it is," Ashante agreed, as a tear flow down her cheek.

They all watched silently as the apparition of the little girl that was Isabella Dupri slowly faded away into the light that now shines brightly thru the boarded-up windows.

"Police!" announces the personnel now entering the house.

Chapter Fifteen

Police and Fire personnel are now on the scene as well as curious neighbors that have gathered around on the sidewalks to see what all the fuss is about in their neighborhood.

"We found what we believe to be the suspect's fake police car parked not too far down from here," Detective Devereaux said.

"And when the Forensics and DNA results come back, I am sure it'll verify that the piece of shit lying on the floor in there is the man we've been looking for," his partner Canty injected.

"Keep me informed," Sam said.

"Will do," Devereaux said. He looked over at Tracy and back at Sam.

"If you two ever consider joining the force let me know," he said with a smile.

"If that's your way of saying thank you, detective, you're welcome," Tracy said.

"Thank you," Devereaux said.

"Meowww," the cat rubbed up against Devereaux's leg.

"I think you've made a friend," Sam said.

"I'll be damn," Devereaux said as he looked down at the cat that now jotted off.

"What?" Sam asked curiously.

Detective Devereaux rubbed his chin stubble in almost disbelief of what he just saw.

"You know that cat had almost the same color eyes that Isabella did."

"Green," Sam said.

And with that said, they all turned around and watched the cat stop and look back at them as if it knew something that they didn't. It yawned and turned the corner and disappeared down the street on its next mission somewhere, maybe nowhere? In the city of New Orleans.

THE END

THE SPELL

ORIGINAL STORY: BY LEE J. MINTER
ARTWORK BY: LEE J. MINTER

CHAPTER ONE

The provocative music was bumping inside a local Las Vegas strip club called *Puss n Booties.* The dancer on the stage seemed like she was in a world of her own as she gyrated her body in sexual positions that were just as titillating as the music she was dancing to. Moves and music that held her captive audience under her spell.

In fact, if one was to evaluate the situation from the outside looking in, they could have come to the simple conclusion, it would not have mattered to her at all if they were not even there. (her captive audience) As long as they left their wallets at the door, and the stage continues to rain dollar bills by some unforeseen force.

The results to her would have been all the same as the song by **Dire Straits,** (Get your) *Money for nothin' in this case tricks for free.*

They were under her spell, and she knew it!

Eyes in the crowd that were full of lust, that hypnotically watch her every move, with erotic thoughts on their minds about just how good she would be in bed? Men with wives, fiancees, girlfriends that were willing to drop their last dollar on their uninhibited fantasies.

A fantasy that most likely would never come true, a fantasy that had the worst betting odds than any Casino in a town, that was built on like - fantasies and lost dreams.

Las Vegas,

The *Rat pack, Elvis, Bugsy Siegel.*

They came, they conquered, and they left.

The dancer who had everyone captivated in the strip club was *Eldorado;* her co-workers called her *Elda* for short.

A very pretty girl of Armenian and African heritage in her mid-twenties with sharp features, long jet black wavy hair, and a lean, curvy body that was a product of her employ and strict vegan diet that she adhered to most times.

Sometimes.

It appeared as if she was levitating down the pole as she executed her signature descent down the top of the pole as if she was walking on air. Her shapely legs outstretched and floating in a synchronicity motion with each other making it appeared her feet were touching stairs that were unseen by the human eye.

The all-black costume she wore or the little of it she was wearing, reminded him of the costumes that Prince's protege Vanity use to wear.

Her long black see thru duster coat swayed in the wind when she walked down the stage like a superhero's cape. It soon came off as she set it down in one corner of the stage, revealing her tight dancer's body to her audience even more explicitly.

Eldorado unsnapped her black laced bra, as easily as if she was drinking a glass of water and tossed it in the same corner with her duster coat. As she cupped her small but firm breasts, pinching the nipples as she teasingly met eye contact with one of the club's frequent patron's a man by the name of Larry Forrester.

Larry watch her as she lifted one of her breasts to her mouth and stroke the nipple with her tongue.

He watched captivated, he watched spellbound.

Eldorado was the only dancer he had come here to see, and it was nothing on this earth he wouldn't do for her.

In contrast, Larry was once a family man that had a nice home, a good job, a loving wife, and two kids that he adored.

Now for reasons, unknown to him that he did not know, nor was he able to explain, he was willing to throw it all away to be with Eldorado, sitting in a dark strip club on the other side of town in Las Vegas eagerly anticipating her arrival.

He could not get her voice out of his head, her scent, her face, that body.

Larry had now spent so much money that should have been going to his family on her, and the strip club, he had lost count.

What had innocently enough started out as a boys night out from work, with his friends had somehow become a full-time addiction to him that he had no control over.

It was like air and water to Larry. He had to be at this particular strip club; he had to see Eldorado, or else he could not eat, sleep, or function thru the day. His wife Allison had noticed the changes in him, subtle at first before they inevitably started to escalate.

Now Larry Forrester found himself sneaking out of the house at odd hours of the night and morning when his family was sleep to be here at *Puss n Boots* with his favorite stripper Eldorado. He found himself making lame ass excuses and telling lame ass lies when his wife questioned him about his whereabouts.

Behavior that in the past had not been characteristic of Larry Forrester.

In fact, Mr. Forrester did not know himself these days at all. When he looked in the mirror at himself lately, it was like looking at an empty vessel of the man that he once was. The dark circles around his puffy eyes were the tell-tale signs that he was sleep deprived, he had lost over thirty pounds in just one month alone and was subsisting off of cigarettes and energy drinks with the occasional upper to keep him afloat and a downer to make him sleep.

His life was literally off the grid of any normalcy he had known before he cast eyes on the seductress he now watched in a hypnotic-like trance named Eldorado.

He had recently emptied out all his bank accounts, investment accounts, joint accounts with his wife, and any future savings that they had set aside for their children's future education, to finance this cancer of an obsession with Eldorado, to provide her with anything that she desired.

Like the Casino's in Las Vegas, she had taken him to the bank and emptied him out. He could make deposits but would not be getting any returns on his investments into her.

As he stared at her in his trance-like state, he reflected on how it all started, how it all began. How she deliciously persuaded him against his better judgment to a private lap dance in one of the V.I.P. rooms in the club.

How Eldorado while mounting his lap and rubbing that beautiful body up against his whispered the words seductively in his ear, "Vous Estes `a moi," (You are mines) in French.

"Je vous possede et Je vous possede," I own you, and I possess you.

He was not literate in French, so how was he suppose to have known? It just sounded good and sexy to him against the beat drop of the provocative music spun by the club's resident deejay.

But he wanted her, and he wanted to possess her also.

But this was Eldorado's house, and like any Casino, the deck was stacked against him. From the time he walked in until the time he walked out.

"Je vous possede et Je vous possede," she whispered in his ear.

"I own you, and I possess you."

And indeed she did. It was now 4:00 am in the morning, and the strip club would soon be closing. Larry knew that Eldorado no longer had any use for him after all his financial resources had run dry.

But he had to have one more lap dance from her, feel the sensation of her beautiful body press up against his when she whispered the last words that he would ever hear from her again, but this time in English.

"You are mine in life, but even more in death."

This time Larry understood perfectly well, every single word that Eldorado had just spoken to him. What directive that she had just given him, as he slowly walked out of the strip club like a zombie, like the broken man he was. He knew now what he had to do, to make all of this right again.

The parking lot to Puss n Bootie's was now desolate except his car that set like an old relic waiting for him to return to its caverns.

Tears now rolled slowly down Larry's face, as he sobbed to himself, as he looked down at the note that he was leaving his family. If he could turn back the hands of time and do things differently, he would have. But that was not the case, and so here he was *decision time.*

Larry placed the note inside an envelope and gently placed it on the front passenger seat next to him. He then drove to an even more desolate area several blocks from the strip club, parked his car.

Larry looked into his rearview mirror at his glazed over eyes that appeared even more zombiesque. He then reached into his glove compartment and pulled out the new 9mm handgun he had just purchased, put the gun to his temple, (smiled) when he heard Eldorado's voice clear as day say "do it!" and blew his brains out all over the car seats all over the - letter.

Back at the club in the dancer's dressing room, Eldorado set at her vanity, cleaning the make-up off her face, preparing to go home.

When suddenly she grabbed her neck and inhaled, as she felt the life leaving out of ex-client Larry Forrester's body. Her eyes appeared to glow red at that very moment as she then proceeded to relax again.

And although the expression on her face was solemn at best, that was not the case of the reflection that looked back at her from the mirror, eyes luminescent red, smiling, with an evil grin on its face.

The image in the mirror faded into the background, faded into darkness, now Eldorado was looking at herself again, at least the image on the surface that she wanted to project.

The lipstick was the last thing to come off, as she tossed the cotton pad in a trash can underneath her vanity desk.

Men are fools she thought.

Lustful fools to be toyed with, played with, and then drained of everything that they had in this world, everything that she could get out of them.

Everything.

She liked the arrangement, or you could say the deal that she had struck up with the owner of the strip club, a flamboyant and nefarious character by the name of Marius Chandelier, part-time pimp, all-time hustler.

Money for souls was her proposal to him. She would make him a wealthy man and in return, let's say he would just let her do her thing.

And boy, would he find out she was good at it, doing her thing that is.

Eldorado he would find out wasn't like (his words) any bitch that had just walked off the streets that now wanted to make a living at the strip game and maybe wanted to sell some occasional pussy on the side.

No, Eldorado was the strip game and made the men and women that came to see her fans forever.

Forever, until she owned them, or until she decided to let them go.

Chandelier you see was unaware that he had made a deal with the devil.

Literally.

He was also unaware that he had made a deal with something as ancient as time itself, made a deal with an enchantress, a demon, a succubus.

And part of that deal that Mr. Marius Chandelier had so reluctantly agreed to with her or "it" was? That he with Eldorado's assistance, of course, would make one human sacrifice a month inside the club.

When the dastardly deed was carried out by the two of them, the victim's body afterward would be cut and sliced up by various tools of the "serial killer trade" he kept hidden on the premises.

The flesh of the victims once separated from their bones would then be boiled, fried or baked depending on what was on Chandelier 's menu that week.

Then unknowingly consumed and cannibalized by the patrons and employees in the club in the form of pastrami sandwiches, hot dogs, chili, pizza garnishments or other imaginative delectables of the flesh sold off a food truck that he ran in the parking lot of his club.

A neckbone in the greens was a neckbone in the greens.

It was a deal with the devil that had made Chandelier a rich man.

The deal; money for souls, souls, for money.

Even his.

Eldorado smiled at the thought that she could not have picked a better place Sin City, Las Vegas, where everything is for sale, and everything has a price.

Sheeple she thought, designed to be led to the slaughter.

Eldorado had been human once, but she too like Chandelier had gotten herself in bed with the devil when her spirit was weak. And when she allowed many of his minions to come into her and take over, the dominant of the many took hold and thus was born Eldorado.

Whenever the house deejay would announce her name before she got on the stage (Eldorado) the whole house would go eerily quiet as all the focus would go to her. She became the club's premier dancer, the main attraction, a star.

Chandelier knew right then that he had himself something special, but how special? He did not know.

The fact that he had pretty much fuck whatever girl he had wanted in the club except her, already made her special in his eyes.

But he did not trust her and for a good reason. Marius Chandelier knew that women like her with the power of persuasion that she had over men and women could be a dangerous thing, because he possessed that same power also, but not to her degree.

That's why he always had the other girls watching Eldorado, watching his back.

Chandelier walked up slowly behind Eldorado in the dressing room and placed his hands on her shoulders. She felt his presence before he had stepped one inch thru the door.

"Good night Elda," he said as he massaged her shoulders.

She knew what he wanted.

"I guess," she said in a nonchalant voice, as she applied another shade of lipstick to her lips.

She peeled Chandelier's hands off her shoulders as she stood up to leave with her purse now slung over her shoulder.

"You are one hot number Elda," he said, as he saliciously looked her up and down with a glint in his eye.

His silk Hawaiian print shirt was hurting her eyes.

"Where did you steal that line from an 80's movie?" she said, as she shoves a roll of cash in his hands.

Her boss Chandelier looks down at the cash with a greedy grin on his face.

"A good night indeed," he says.

He takes his finger and strokes her left shoulder with it gently.

"How about you and me celebrate," he asks.

"I would, but I might break you," Eldorado says as she removes Chandelier finger from off her arm.

"Ouch, don't be so rough," Chandelier says playfully.

"Anyway, I need you to keep your mind on business and not my pussy understood?" Elda said, firmly with a tone in her voice Chandelier did not like.

"Trust me, I can do both," Chandelier shot back.

Eldorado smiled at him, to her Chandelier was just a grown insecure little boy that wanted her to make him feel like a man. Unfortunately for him, she was not up for that task.

"I bet you can, but don't forget the arrangement we have, you keep up your end of the bargain I'll keep up mines, understand?"

Chandelier slowly nodded his head yes, in defeat.

"Good, now stop aiming so high and go and fuck one of those stupid tramps out there," she said, Chandelier eyes narrowed.

"You know you're starting to talk to me like you're my boss," he said angrily.

"How else am I suppose to talk to you?" Eldorado snapped back.

"If I wanted you to lick the crack of a hobo's ass, do you think you could resist? Do you!" Eldorado shouted out.

Chandelier stood frozen as he watched her face begin to change and take on a monstrous appearance, her pupils become red pinpoints.

"Do you?" she asked again this time in a deeper more masculine voice.

Chandelier responded nervously with a stutter "You wouldn't make me li.. li.. lick a hobo's ass would you?"

"Either that or you could be his bitch for the day, that Hawaiian silk shirt would make a nice mini dress Marius," she said bluntly.

"Are you starting to get the picture Marius Chandelier?" Eldorado added her face now back to a human appearance.

"Loud and clear," Chandelier answered nervously.

"Good now stay in your lane," Eldorado said, as she walked out the dressing room.

Chandelier remains silent as he watches her leave, he was right that crazy bitch or whatever that thing was *masquerading* as a human was *extremely dangerous*!

Why had he gone this far he thought, and what was he thinking?

He now begins to realize no amount of money in the world was worth the hell he had created for himself.

There was though a way out of this he reasoned, how could he destroy it soon? Before "it" decided he was no longer of any use and came after him first.

Chapter Two

Eldorado was aware that she had a lot of eyes on her, on and off the dance floor, and that one pair of those eyes belonged to a co-worker and dancer that went by the stage name Misty Grant.

Misty was one of the few girls that she was close to in the club on a personal level and one that Chandelier had requested that she take under her wing and tutelage as a protégé.

And although Misty was a pretty and shapely girl in her own right, Chandelier knew that she lacked the enigmatic qualities that Eldorado possessed, but she would at least make a good spy he thought. But unknown to him Eldorado had already suspected as much but chose to go along with the program as if she was oblivious to this fact.

"Keep your friends close, but your enemies closer," was after all one of her "mottos" that she had made her own. The "little girl" as she termed (Misty) was not only a mortal but a novice to her, so she fed her what she wanted to feed her as far as information.

Information that was impertinent to Eldorado and just enough to keep Marius Chandelier baited and happy.

In fact, the only thing that she would miss about Misty Grant in case she had to dispose of her in the bed, that they had shared on numerous occasions together, she had to admit she liked the way Misty felt in her mouth, soft, supple, and warm.

But if she had to get rid of the bitch, she thought, Misty like the rest of them, once she had gone thru the "meat grinder" would make a nice pastrami sandwich on rye bread served a la carte.

Eldorado licked her lips wet at the thought, as she set her sight on her next victim in the strip club, a middle age man with a prominent bald spot that he unsuccessfully tried to cover up with a combover and some hairspray.

But she could also see that he was dress very nicely and that his polyester pants might contain more than just his excitement at the various dancers, that took turns displaying their assets and wares on the stage and the pole.

The patron set at a table with a small entourage of his own as Eldorado walked over to join him upon his request.

"How it's going tonight handsome?" she asked him as she walked up to his table, zoning in on him and picking him out of the other three men in his group. He looked her up and down as he took her by the hand that she had offered him. "Fine doll, now that you're here," he said.

"Have a seat," he offered.

Eldorado set down on his lap; she could feel the other men at his table watching her and him with envy like grinning hyenas.

"Hot damn! You're gorgeous what's your name beautiful?" he asked.

"Eldorado," she answered.

"Like the fabled city of gold?" he asked.

"Who says it's a fable," rebutted Eldorado.

Her *mark* laughed, revealing overly white teeth if there was such a thing.

"Is there gold down there?" he asked, as his eyes went down between her legs towards the black g-string that she was wearing.

"Would you like to find out?" she whispered in his ear.

"Oh boy would I," he replied with a big grin on his face revealing those too white teeth again.

Eldorado massages his arm causing his sleeve to go up revealing a nice Rolex Cellini watch on his wrist.

She smiled as she mentally noted that his one wrist alone was worth at least fifteen thousand dollars. She was right about Mr. Polyester pants he had more than just an erection in his slacks, he had deep pockets, and she for one did not mind burying her hands deep inside of them.

It was time to start digging.

"Would you like a private dance in the v.i.p. room," she asked.

"Show me the way," he said cheerfully, as he picked up his drink off the table.

Several other girls had now joined his friends at their table to the party, so his "associates" were now too distracted by the other skimpily clad vixens around them to worry about what the hell their friend was doing or where the hell he was going.

Eldorado took Mr. Polyester pants by the hand and guided him to the VIP room. That would be the last that they would be seeing their friend for the rest of the night.

The last time they would see him again.

Back in the v.i.p. room in a more intimate setting Eldorado now slid her upper naked body down Mr. Polyester pants exposed chest as she straddles him.

He sat back with his mouth agape and his eyes glazed over a ghastly white.

"Je vous possede et Je vous possede," she whispered in his ear.

I own you, and I possess you.

Chapter Three

Chandelier fastens the watch onto his wrist. "Nice Rolex," he said out loud, to himself, admiring the timepiece. He then took a handkerchief out of his pocket and wiped a speck of blood off of the glass face of the watch. "Aaaahhh, much better now," he said holding his wrist up towards the light.

Eldorado observed him from across the room, the strip club was now empty besides the three of them, and the bloody parts of a mutilated body cut up in various pieces like meat from a butcher shop on a large plastic tarp sprawled out on the back kitchen floor.

It is this part of the bargain (the killing and dismemberment) is what Chandelier soon detested the most.

Murder.

To him, Eldorado had now made him an unwitting accomplice to her succession of murders, and insatiable appetite for bloodlust, thus making him into (he wanted to vomit whenever he thought of this) a fucking serial killer.

He took the watch off and put it back in his jacket pocket underneath the plastic apron that he wore.

Eldorado stuffed the polyester pants with the other remnants of clothing from the victim into a small garbage bag, all of this with his bones in another bag would go to dumping sites familiar to only her and Chandelier.

She calmly smoked a cigarette as she surveyed her and Chandelier's handy work.

"Hey, no need to be squeamish he won't bite back I can assure you that," she said sarcastically.

Chandelier wiped the sweat off of his forehead as he contemplated the grisly task ahead of them.

"Put the bones in the bag and the meat in the grinder," Eldorado said.

"I know, put the bones in the bag and the meat in the grinder," Chandelier repeated.

"You don't have to tell me twice," he said angrily, as he tossed a limb into one of the garbage bags, nervously eyeing the gruesome sight of the victim's headless upper torso on the tarp.

"Are you forgetting something?" Eldorado asked as she pointed out to Chandelier a gold and black ring with the initials MC on one of severed hands fingers. "Oh shit, I didn't see that!" Chandelier picked up the severed hand and tugged at the ring to remove it from the finger, but despite his attempts, it would not come off the finger that it was attached too.

Eldorado quickly snatched the hand away from Chandelier, tossed it on the kitchen counter and in the blink of an eye swiftly cut off the finger with a meat cleaver that she held in her other hand.

Eldorado pulled the ring off the bloody finger and tossed it to Chandelier. "See how easy that was," she said with a smirk.

Chandelier caught the ring and went to stuff it in his pocket but in his nervous ridden haste missed the inside of his pocket; the ring went tumbling unnoticed by him or Eldorado to the floor with a ping.

It was hot as hell in the back kitchen, and he just wanted to be done with this task and move on, it would be another month until she or it would demand another sacrifice, which was fine by him.

The rank smell of blood and guts filled his nostrils, as he wiped the sweat from his forehead leaving a smudge of blood in its place. He could not understand how Eldorado could be so detached? Was never nervous, never broke a sweat or batted an eye while she carried out these heinous murders and dismemberments.

Yes, technically he had never murdered any of the victims, although he had been a willing participant in the latter. Not that it would have mattered much to the police if they had discovered what he and his discompassionate co-part had been up too.

Bang bang bang! The loud knock at the front door startled them both or at least him. "What the fuck now?" he said underneath his breath.

"Diesel see who is at the gotdamn front door will ya?" he screamed out at the large doorman and bouncer that was in the front area of the club.

"Sure boss!" he heard his employee scream back at him from the front.

"We need to get this shit bagged up and out of here," Eldorado said.

"Shit!" Chandelier blurted out as he watched wide-eyed as his bouncer came crashing thru the kitchen double doors with a shotgun pressed up to the back of his head, accompanied by three-man, which included the guy with the shotgun to his noggem.

"Sorry boss," he said nervously.

"It's okay Diesel," Chandelier said to him.

Eldorado recognized the three men right away; they were the ones sitting at the table earlier.

"What the fuck is going on in here?" shouted out one of the goons as he looked at the bloody scene.

"It looks like these sick fucks done had themselves a party," said his friend.

"Drop the meat cleaver bitch! And the both of you need to get those hands in the air," the first one that had made the inquiry ordered, he appeared to be the leader out of the three.

Colorado dropped the meat cleaver to the floor which made a loud clanging noise as it made contact.

"I recognize her, she was the one that came to the table for Mike," said goon number two.

"I think you got me mistaken," Eldorado said firmly.

"Bitch! you calling me a liar?" he rebutted.

"I am saying you're mistaken," she said, holding her ground.

"Who is this on the floor?" the leader demanded to know.

" Trust me he's no one that you should be concern about," Chandelier said.

The words had almost not fully left his mouth before he got a quick smack across the lips with Goon number one's pistol instantly splitting it and drawing blood.

"Motherfucker we are not here to play games!" he said.

"We are looking for our friend Mike, he did not go home, and the last place we saw him was here," said the leader.

"We don't know your friend Mister, and if he came with you he should have left with you," Chandelier said, as he wiped the blood off his lip.

"Yeah that's the only thing you got right asshole," the leader said, as he looked over at his other associate with the shotgun to the bouncers head. A slight nod was all his trigger man needed, as their eyes met.

And just like that, he let loose with the shotgun, Blam!

The bouncer's brains were all over the kitchen floor, the big man's body dropped face forward, with a loud thud to the floor, revealing a now large and gaping hole to the back of his head. A whiff of blueish gunsmoke creeps up out of the wound and into the air.

Chandelier and Eldorado jumped back startled by the brazen execution of the bouncer and doorman.

Chandelier looked on in shock; it was the first time that he had seen Eldorado respond emotionally to anything, maybe she still had some human left in her after all he reasoned.

"Now do you think we are serious?" the leader asked them un empathetically.

Goon two smiled.

"Now unless you two twisted fucks want to join your friend "Dead engine" here on the floor, I advise one of you to start talking and quick."

In all of the chaos that had ensued, no one had noticed that Eldorado had discreetly slid the meat cleaver that was in front of her, behind her with her foot when no one was looking.

Goon two eyes went over to the metal table to the severed hand and the chop off fingers of the victim, one of them pointing in Eldorado's direction.

The leader of the group eyes went straight to Eldorado, it was something about this broad he did not like but just couldn't put his finger on it right now.

"Hey man check that out!" Goon two said to his two friends while motioning to the table.

"The finger saying the bitch did it."

Goon three held the shotgun on Chandelier and Eldorado, ready to drop them like a bad habit, at the least sign of aggression by either one of them. His expressionless face and intense glare said it all "Move, and I'll blow your fucking brains out all over this place!"

"Maybe a message from the grave?" the leader said, staring dryly.

Yes, he knew what it was now, it was something about her eyes that he did not like, they almost seemed to him, that if you stared into them too long, they could hypnotize you put a spell on yo…

"Hey you, pick that up off the floor!" his associate wielding the shotgun ordered Chandelier to do after he spotted what looked like a piece of jewelry.

Chandelier looked down at the spot that the gunman had pointed his weapon and that is when he saw the ring that he thought he had put in his pocket, lying on the floor. A lump suddenly forms in his throat that he is unable to swallow.

"Slowly genius," the leader said with his weapon aimed at Chandelier.

Chandelier reached down slowly as instructed and pick up the black and gold ring off the bloody kitchen floor.

"Toss it to me."

Goon number one (the leader) caught the ring in his free hand and wiped the blood off of it with his fingers, as he held it up for close inspection. It was a familiar piece of jewelry that he had seen before, two spades on each side of it and the initials MC in gold on a black onyx background.

This ring could belong to only one person that he knew of, his boss and friend a mobster by the name of Mike Castellini.

But he wanted to be for sure before he took the next step.

"What did you say your name was bub?"

"I didn't but its Marius Chandelier." Did he call me bub? Marius thought.

"Is this your ring ten-watt?" the leader asked.

"Yes."

"Describe it to me."

"It has my initials MC in gold on a black background Mister; it was a gift from my daughter."

Eldorado watched quietly at everything that was playing out, and every time one of the goons took her eyes off of her, she eased herself closer to the light switch on the wall panel next to her, as she slid the meat cleaver behind her, along her path.

“Is that all?” was his final question.

Chandelier looked back at him with anxiety and a sense of warranted dread; maybe he had a way out of this mess after all.

‘Yeah, and it was all of that bitch over there idea,” he said, pointing over to Eldorado.

His interrogator smiled as he tossed his friend goon two the ring.

“That’s all,” said the leader.

Goon two looked at it, smiled, raised his gun to Chandelier’s head and pulled the trigger.

Chandelier brain matter flew out the side of his head before he hit the floor dead.

Click, the lights then went out in the kitchen leaving them in complete darkness. Bang bang bang bang bang. Rapid gunshots now let loose as muzzle flash from the three goons guns lit up the darkness in the kitchen.

“Stop shooting you fucking morons, before you kill us all!” shouted out Goon number one.

The gunfire ceased, followed by a scream of pain and agony by one of his associate’s Goon number two, as Eldorado surgically implanted a meat cleaver in the middle of his forehead, he fell to the floor cross-eyed, convulsed for a few seconds, and died.

Goon number three was able to find the light switch and flip it back on, but not before Eldorado swiftly came across his throat with a butcher knife severing his trachea. He reactively dropped his shotgun and grabbed his throat to stop the bleeding.

Goon number one watched on in shock as the blood squirted between his friend's fingers as he tried to speak. He put him to rest with a bullet to the head, after firing several shots at Eldorado and missing.

He stuffed his semi-auto pistol in his pocket and picked up Goon number three's shotgun as he proceeds out of the kitchen to the front of the strip club. This psycho bitch had dropped two of his best men he thought, and he was going to make sure she paid with her life.

They had underestimated her (his men) and paid dearly with their lives, he promised himself, as he made his way thru the club searching for her, he would not make that same mistake.

Pumping a slug into the shotgun, he cautiously scans the dimly lit club when dance music suddenly starts playing from the clubs speaker system "startling him" causing him to spin around towards the DJ booth.

He lets loose with the shotgun blowing a hole thru one of the clubs walls.

"Folks and all non-believers get ready for the hypnotizing and mesmerizing Eldorado," a voice says over the music.

"What the fuck?" Goon one says to himself, as he now watches Eldorado walk slowly out on the stage in black lingerie and a duster coat to the beat of the music.

Whomever the mysterious voice belongs to is right, she is one of the most stunning women he has ever laid eyes on, why hadn't he recognized that at first sight, he wonders? But this is fucking crazy he thinks, he wants to kill her, wants to make her pay for what she has done to his friends.

Her eyes meet his as he lowers his shotgun, she puts her finger in that lovely pouty mouth of hers, never breaking eye contact with him, as her body sways rhythmically back and forth to the beat of the music. The duster coat comes off exposing more of her lean voluptuous body, as he imagines being inside of her, taking her in his mouth.

Eldorado slowly removes her bra exposing breast that even Venus De Milo would be envious of, as she slowly gyrates to the music as she wraps her body around the dance pole like a charmed viper.

She now climbs up the pole maneuvering and flipping her body down with the gymnastic skill of a seasoned veteran, her legs spread wide and body perfectly arch as she descends the metal phallic between her legs.

She dismounts off the pole to the pulsating beat of the music, as her only customer Goon number one, fights the urge not to keep his eyes on her, its as if she is taking over his thoughts, taking over his mind.

"What the fuck is she?" he says to himself.

The stage and the front of the club suddenly go dark.

Goon one snaps out of it quick enough to catches a glimpse of the shadow of something running quickly up the wall and behind him making guttural noises.

Staring up at the wall, he cannot believe what is looking down at him.

A bat like a creature with white pinpoints eyes that glow in the dark and the tail of a serpent, extending down from underneath its muscular legs.

It releases itself from the wall and comes down at him, with an ear-piercing shriek, with something shiny and pointy in its hand; Goon one lets loose the pump, blowing a hole thru the demon, as the blast from the shotgun propels the creature back off of him and onto the floor.

It makes those weird guttural sounds as he approaches it, but this time it's different as if it's struggling to breathe.

Goon number one pumps another round unmercifully into the twisted winged abomination struggling to breathe on the club's floor.

Silence.

Chapter Four

Vinnie watches from a distance, as flames engulf a seedy strip joint that he just set on fire, called *Puss n Booties* per order of the Boss. He listens to the fire engines now fast approaching in the distance, to no doubt put out his five-alarm masterpiece.

He throws the cigarette and the pastrami sandwich wrapper down to the ground, extinguishing the cigarette bud with his foot. Walks around to the back of his cargo van, looks at the three bodies of his deceased associates and closes the back doors to the van.

From here on out he concludes strip clubs is definitely off his radar, especially the ones in Las Vegas.

Two months later somewhere on the east side of Atlanta, GA at a local strip club called *The Crave.*

The music is bumping as the Deejay sets the pace for the night and the main attraction that everyone inside the club has been waiting for and anticipating.

He begins his announcement: "We have a very special treat for you tonight folks, this beautiful creature is in a league of her own, put your hands together for the hypnotizing, and mesmerizing

Eldorado."

THE END

PIPER SHIPPING

BLIND DATE

ORIGINAL STORY: BY LEE J. MINTER
ARTWORK BY: LEE J. MINTER

Chapter One

A tall and handsome gentleman by the name of Jonathan Piper looks at a pic of the blind date on his cell phone that he has arranged to meet at a night spot and tavern in downtown Chicago, called Logan's.

He scrolls thru the list of other potential suitors on the dating and hook-up app on his phone, different faces of women, with different profiles.

"The twenty-first century does have its perks," he says to himself with a sly grin on his face, as he enters Logan's leaving the cold chill of the December wind behind him on the slushy streets of Chicago.

Jonathan flashes that one-hundred-watt smile of his, as he spots his date sitting at one of the corner tables by herself. A smile that he had mastered to turn on and off at will, to disarm the most cautious of women.

As a successful businessman and investor, not only did Jonathan Piper look the part but was the part you see, and had no problem displaying his wealth and appreciation for the finer things in life.

Such as the pretty young thing he duly noted to himself, as he entered the bar where she sat by herself in the corner of the tavern.

He walked over to the table and kindly introduce himself to his blind date. “Hi, I am Jonathan Piper you must be…” “Laura yes,” she said nervously interrupted him.

“Sorry,” Laura said apologetically, after recognizing that she had cut Jonathan off in mid-sentence.

“No, it's quite alright may I have a seat, Laura.”

“Please do,” she said,” nodding towards the empty chair. Jonathan took off his dark trench coat and draped it over one of the three empty chairs at the table.

Laura could now see that Jonathan was an impeccable dresser, his European dark grey suit with an open white collar shirt fitted his athletic build like, he was a Greek god. She was also sure that anyone looking from afar with the least sense of a fashion acumen, could tell his taste was tailor made and not tailor rack.

She now wonders if he was way above her social and economic status for her to even consider dating a man of this caliber. Wait what was she saying? Was she now not guilty of doing what she would not want anyone else to do to her, judging a book by its cover, she thought?

At the very least with more forethought, she reasoned, she could at least give him the benefit of the doubt, before classifying him as a rich snob fraternizing below his pay grade.

“Wow, you are indeed a very lovely woman Laura,” Jonathan said to her with a smile.

“ Thank you and so are you,” she said.

“What?” he laughed.

"Oh I am sorry, I meant a very handsome man," she said now even more embarrassed than she was before.

If she kept making a faux pas like this, she thought all night; it was no way that she was going to make a connection with Mr. Right.

"No worries, I knew what you meant," he said, with that one-hundred-watt smile, which did not go unnoticed by Laura.

"I hope that I didn't embarrass you by my compliment? he said.

"And why would you say that?" Laura asked curiously.

"Because it has been my experience, that most people seldom resemble their internet profile, you exceed it."

"Thanks again Jonathan, but I feel there is something that I must share with you before this date proceeds on," Laura said.

"Can it please wait for now Laura, I have something as well, I would like to share with you, but I would like our evening together, for now, to be spent on getting to know the inner person and not just what's on the outside okay?" Jonathan politely requested.

"Fair enough, but I still have something to tell you, if not now, later," Laura said, reluctantly agreeing to his terms for now.

The server came over and inquired if they wanted anything to drink.

"I'll take a Gin & Tonic thank you," Laura said.

"And a Bloody Mary for me with extra salt please," Jonathan added.

"I'll get those drinks to you guy's right away," the server said with a smile.

"Thank you," Jonathan said.

"A Bloody Mary that's an interesting choice, you wouldn't be fighting off a hangover would you?" Laura asked.

"I am indeed, from work."

"I see, and what type of work do you do?"

"I am an investor and a software developer for medical applications," Jonathan answered.

"Wow, how exciting! Is there anything that isn't top secret that you are presently working on in regards to medical applications that you can tell me about?" Laura asked curiously.

"One Gin & Tonic and one Bloody Mary," interrupted the server as she set the drinks down in front of them.

"Thanks," they both said.

Laura took a sip of her Gin & Tonic out of the cocktail glass while still waiting for the answer to her earlier question.

Her date Jonathan not to be upstaged followed suit with his drink.

"Aaaahhh, extra salt just the way I like it," he said with a look of satisfaction on his face, as he pops one of the olives in his mouth that was impaled on a long cocktail skewer pick inside his drink.

He could feel Laura eyes watching him curiously as he took a sip of his drink.

"Oh' in regards to your question Laura I am presently working on a software application that may be used in the future to preserve the lifespan of donor blood."

"How impressive," Laura said.

"And what is the current lifespan of stored blood outside of the body?"

"Forty-two days at the most," Jonathan answered.

"And what are you shooting for?"

"Now that my dear is top secret," Jonathan said with a grin on his face.

"By the way did we forget something?" he asked Laura.

Laura looks on puzzled at first and then it came to her that Jonathan was referring to her second faux pax for tonight.

She raised her glass in the air. "What are we toasting to?" she said.

"Whatever you want," Jonathan said.

"Whatever we want?" Laura repeated flirtatiously back to her handsome date.

"To life, love, and blood!" she said cheerfully.

"I can drink to that," Jonathan said tossing back some more of his Bloody Mary.

He patted his mouth afterward with his table napkin leaving a light stain of red on the napkin that he set back down on the table.

Laura like the way his lips curved, she wondered how they would feel on the nipples of her breast?

"I think your profile said you were in the Insurance business, am I correct Laura?"

"Yes, but obviously it does not compare to what you are doing."

"I am sure your job is just as important, just in a different aspect," he assured Laura, flashing that hundred watt smile.

"What kind of Insurance do you sell?" he asked.

"What kind do you need Home, Auto, Boat, life?" she said, trying not to sound too much like a damn television commercial.

"The kind that will assure me that if I ever get sick, I'll get the key to your heart," he said.

Laura looked into his eyes for a moment and smiled before bursting out in laughter.

"What?" Jonathan asked, smiling at Laura's reaction.

"That was so fucking corny but hot at the same time," she said, still laughing.

"Thanks, I try my worst, I guess?" Jonathan said laughing.

He liked the way Laura's mouth formed when she laughed, how those high cheekbones in her face set when she showed expressions of happiness.

But most of all he liked the way she smelled, which made him wonder about how she would taste in his mouth when it was time for her to willingly give herself over to him when she would allow him to give himself to her uninhibited.

Would she be excited, nervous, passionate? Or all of the above when she gave him the key to her lotus flower he thought.

Laura leaned across the table and gave him a gentle peck on the lips. "I like you, Jonathan Piper," she said softly, trying to read his reaction to what she had just done.

"I like you too Laura," he said, as he leaned back in for a kiss that this time lasted much longer than the one she gave him.

He was right; she did taste good.

Wait she thought, what has she done? Laura had not planned on it going this far. She had to tell him the truth before this date went any further.

She had to let him know about herself no matter how painful the process might be. She had to let him know now! And not later.

"Look, Jonathan, its something I need to share with you before we go any further with this tonight," Laura said.

"You don't have to tell me anything, I already know," he said.

"You already know?" Laura asked stunned.

But how could he? She thought. Had she been that obvious, or was he one of those guy's that had a fetish for women like her?

Jonathan took her by the hand.

"Look, Laura, I don't care about the person you were in the past, I care about the person you are now, do you understand?" he said.

Laura looked into Jonathan's eyes and saw something about them that she wondered why she had not noticed it before? That despite his handsome face, they were strange eyes.

Strange eyes, that almost seem to have a hypnotic glow to them. But eyes that seem to have an understanding of the universe, an understanding of who and what Laura was about in the past and the present, and maybe even in the future.

"I understand," she said softly, touching his face almost in a hypnotic state of mind.

Jonathan took her hand and gently kiss the palm of it, his lips felt soft, Laura thought, against her skin.

"Are you enjoying yourself, Laura?" Jonathan wanted to know.

"I think I would enjoy myself better if the ambiance were a little more private," Laura answered with a mischievous twinkle in her eye.

"I see, how private?" Jonathan inquired.

"Private," whispered Laura in his ear.

"I think I can arrange that," Jonathan said with a look of satisfaction on his face. He then removes his cell phone from his coat, calls his chauffeur and orders him to meet them outside in the front of Logan's.

Shortly after Jonathan makes his phone call, a large gentleman of Indian descent dressed in a chauffeur's uniform appears at the front entrance of Logan's.

The chauffeur waves in Jonathan's direction, Jonathan to Laura appears to know the hulking figure; He sees the somewhat distress look in Laura's eyes.

"Don't worry about him he's just a big teddy bear," he assures her.

They both make their way towards the front door held open by his driver.

As they both exit the bar the cold wind off the Chicago river makes Laura snuggle into her coat even more.

Now Laura begins to worry that maybe she has made a bad decision leaving with a guy she barely knows. As Laura looks up her mouth drops open.

A black gleaming Rolls Royce Phantom is parked in front of them, waiting like a chariot for them to enter inside its cavern.

"Is that your car?" Laura asks a bit overwhelm.

"Yes, one of them," Jonathan replied as if it's no big deal with his one hundred watt smile.

"Impressive," she says.

"Yeah, a little bit," Jonathan says with a grin.

"Thank you, Iman," he says to his chauffeur standing by the cars massive suicide doors (backward hinged) as he and Laura enter a car that she knows probably cost more than her Chicago lakefront condo.

As Laura sits down in the cars luxurious seat, she discovers that the car's opulence does not stop at the exterior.

Iman pushes a button on the doors hinges and the massive vaulted doors automatically close shut on the beast.

How rich is this guy? Laura begins to wonder as she gazes above at the multitude of sparkling fiber-optic stars on the headliner of the car.

Chapter Two

The mammoth size automobile powered by a 6.75-liter V12 engine rolls down the city streets of Chicago effortlessly towards the Southside of Chicago to a warehouse owned by Jonathan Piper on Belden St.

As they arrive at their location, Laura is now a little more at ease with the situation, courtesy of the expensive Champagne from the car's fold-out bar "no doubt" she concludes.

But the creepy surroundings that Jonathan's driver has now pulled into, with the mortgage note on wheels has not evaded her sixth sense.

"Why are we here?" she asks Jonathan.

"This is my home Laura," Jonathan states in a voice as if she should have already known.

"What were you expecting a mansion?" he jokes trying to put her at ease.

Laura looks out of the tinted windows at the massive warehouse, she heard about stories like "this" how women against their better judgment allowed themselves to be taken to desolate locations by their blind dates only never to be seen from anyone, ever, again.

She did not want to be one of those women.

"I don't know what I was expecting?" she said after a long pause.

"Laura, I can have my driver take you home if you wish?" Jonathan said, with a look on his face that told her he was fine with whatever decision she made.

A voice in Laura's head suddenly intervene, it was her voice "Why are you hesitating to be adventurous Laura, is he not the man of your dreams?"

"How are you going to live life if you never take chances?"

A second voice intervenes in her head overtaking the first, but this time it was not her's, it belongs to her late Mother's who had passed away recently due to illness.

"Be careful Laura, not everyone will take the time to understand; I love you."

Her mother's voice fades from her head, replaced by the sound of Jonathan's voice.

"Laura are you okay?"

"Yes, why are we still sitting here in this car?" she asks smiling and trying to regain the confidence that she had before they left the bar.

Jonathan leans in and kisses Laura softly on her lips. "Yes, why are we?" he says with a grin.

His chauffeur Iman turns around and looks at his boss.

Jonathan winks his eye at him letting him know its okay to continue inside the warehouse that he calls his home.

The chauffeur hits a button in the car which activates one of the numerous wide warehouse metal garage doors, that begin to raise up allowing them entry to the warehouse. The buzzing of the door rumbling back on its rails and wheels fill the night air on Belden St.

The Rolls Royce Phantom creeps slowly into the warehouse.

Laura and Jonathan exit the vehicle and he bids his large chauffeur Iman farewell, giving him the rest of the night off.

Laura watches intently as the mortgage on wheels exit the low lit warehouse and the rolling metal garage door closes.

"You live in a warehouse?" she says to Jonathan befuddle, as she pulls her coat in from the cold draft that comes from the expansive area of the almost empty warehouse, that looks to be at least two football fields long or more to her.

"Yes I do, I know some people may find it strange, but trust me its more to this place then meets the eye," he assures her with a sense of unapologetic confidence or is it swagger, that she found alluring and disarming.

" Well I guess on the bright side you will never run out of closet space," Laura she said feeling now a little apprehensive.

"No, its plenty of space to throw shit out where ever you want around here," Jonathan said with a grin on his face.

A comment that Laura could not help but find slightly disturbing given the circumstances.

"Would you like me to show you around?"

"Please do," answer Laura, trying to hide her nervousness from her new acquaintance while putting her bravest face on to contradict the "willy nillies" in her stomach.

"Please come this way," Jonathan requested politely, as he took Laura by the hand. Laura noticed a small golf cart parked over in one of the corners of the warehouse.

"Are we going to be needing that?" she asked, pointing over to the golf cart.

"Not yet, unless you plan on escaping?" he said sarcastically.

Laura smiled slightly at Jonathan's remark, but in her head, the thought of being held a prisoner in this warehouse or any warehouse for that matter did not sit well with her at all.

In fact, she had made a mental note of three possible exits out of the place in case things went south.

The two of them walked over to a large double black vault door with a multitude of gold decorative inserts inside its frame, and a gargoyle head mounted in the middle of its center.

Laura watched in amazement as Jonathan place his thumb on a Biometric access control reader mounted on the side of the door.

The scanner makes a buzzing noise as it lights up in a neon blue and then unlocks the door.

"Impressive," she says underneath her breath as her eyes go back to the gargoyle head on the center of the door.

Laura's eyes go wide again, as the two doors electronically open by themselves revealing a spacious and nicely decorated upscale loft with a fireplace and wet bar.

"You were right it is more to this place than meets the eye," she says.

Jonathan assists Laura with removing her coat and hangs it up on one of the coat hooks mounted on his wall.

Laura walks over to the fireplace to warm herself rubbing her hands together.

Jonathan watches her closely.

"Can I fix you a drink, Laura?"

"Thanks," she responds, as she begins to warm up.

"Gin and Tonic."

"Of course," she says as she makes her way over to the wet bar.

The life-size samurai statue in one corner of the room in full combat armor with sword catches Laura's eye.

"That's a nice piece of Japanese art you have there."

"Oh' that old thing, I've had it for ages I purchase it from a antiquities dealer some time ago in Lousiana, a gentleman with a very unusual name."

Jonathan passes Laura, the Gin &Tonic he has made for her across the bar.

"Oh' now I remember, I believe his name was "*Solo Chase*," he said.

"That is unusual," Laura agreed.

"How's your drink?"

"Delicious," Laura said, as she sucks on the piece of lime that garnished her drink.

Her Mother's voice enters Laura's head again " Be careful Laura; not everyone will take the time to understand, I love you."

"I have something I think I should tell you before we go any further with this Jonathan."

"No more talking," Jonathan says as he comes from around the bar, takes Laura in his strong arms and passionately kisses her in the mouth. She reciprocates his action, as her tongue searches the inside of his warm mouth.

Jonathan pushes the bar chairs aside and turns Laura around with her back now facing him. She takes off her panties, sliding them off down her legs.

Jonathan unzips his pants and raises her dress up as he moistens his fingers with his saliva. Laura feels the titillating wetness from his fingers on her as she arches her ass in the air ready to receive him, ready to take all of him inside of her.

Laura is tighter then he imagines she would be, as he attempts to enter inside of her, but something does not feel quite right. Despite this his canine teeth begin to become elongated as he sinks them into the side of Laura's neck, blood begin to form, she feels their sharpness, the pain.

"No, Stop!" she screams out.

Jonathan ignores her and continues despite her objection!

Laura manages to grabs a decanter bottle off of the bar filled with whiskey and smashes it across Jonathan's head.

The blow stuns him, knocking him to the ground.

"What's wrong with you? I said stop you fucking asshole!" she shouts out to him infuriated.

She watches as he grabs the top of his head, the dark blood gushing out from his wound all over his white shirt as he attempts to get back his composure.

"What were you trying to do, rape me?" Laura asks, still holding the empty decanter now with his blood on it in one hand.

Jonathan now begins to laugh, and it is the most sinister thing that Laura has ever heard before in her life, a laugh that now lets her know she has made the wrong decision to go with this stranger.

Jonathan looks up smiling at her with blood on his face, with a maniacal expression on her face she did not recognize.

"Oh no" I want to kill you! He said calmly, as he flashed that one hundred watt smile of his, that one hundred watt smile now filled with vampire-like teeth.

The glass decanter came across his head again, this time exploding into glass splinters knocking him back down as he attempted to get up.

Just then Laura heard a buzzing noise in the room, and look over just in time to notice that the double black vaulted doors in the room were closing!

She quickly grabbed her coat off of the nearby hanger and dashed towards the doors barely squeezing her way thru it's narrowing opening before they finally close shut on her with a loud bang.

"Crazy muthafucker," Laura said underneath her breath, as she attempts to get some of her composure back.

Laura looks back up at the gargoyle head staring at her on the door. If it could have spoken she was sure it would have said to her "What did you expect was going to happen behind black and gold doors with a gargoyle head mounted on it?"

"Fuck you!" Laura said as she gave it the middle finger.

Suddenly a beep came from the door as the Biometric access control reader lit up in its neon blue.

Laura froze in terror as she watched the door begin to creak open slowly.

"Snap out of it Laura!" her deceased mother's voice demanded.

Between the gap in the door, Laura could now see Jonathan staring at her with a fanged grin on a monstrous alabaster face with red pupils, that hone in on her like laser dots. Gone was the handsome mask that this creature of the night had worn earlier at the tavern.

Laura watched in a state of immobilization, as her body froze up on her.

She attempts to move but is unable to move a muscle in her catatonic state of fear.

"Snap out of it Laura, run now!" her mother's voice screamed.

The creature would be free soon as the door gap continues to widen.

"You must move now Laura, move!" her mother's voice beckoned.

Laura closes her eyes and begins to concentrate on breaking herself free from her state of immobility.

Laura suddenly feels the bottom of her feet becoming unglued from the floor, and with a tug and a little effort she breaks free and makes a dash for one of the exits that she had seen earlier.

A cold breeze blew over her neck as she ran for her life towards one of the warehouse exits and instinctively she knew Jonathan was not far behind.

Not far behind her, shit! She thought as she froze in her tracks.

Laura could now see that he had somehow manifested himself in front of her, and was headed in her direction.

Laura quickly ducked behind some wooden shipping crates that were stacked about eight feet high. She noticed a crowbar on the floor next to the crates, and that is when she got the idea that if she could slide the crowbar underneath one of them, she could shift it enough to create an avalanche effect.

The problem was she knew the success of this idea all rest upon the weight of the crates, and if could she shift it.

The vampirish creature who used to be Jonathan walked slowly and methodically towards the direction of Laura, sniffing the air for its prey, like a wild animal, it could smell her scent, smell her blood.

Laura jams the crowbar underneath the wooden crate and begins to pull up on it with all the strength she could summon up in her body.

At first, the crate barely bulges, but to her amazement, she feels it shifts a little forward then a little more until the top crate rocks back and forth towards Laura as if it's going to fall.

"Shit!" she blurts out as she jumps out the way, alerting the creature now of her whereabouts. The creature reacts to the sound of her voice, moving towards her direction, but it's too late for it to move out the way as the wooden crates come tumbling down on top of its head on top of its body.

Laura lies on the concrete floor with her hands over her head waiting for the crates to pummel her but they never do, she hears them crash to the floor, but she is unaware of where they have fallen.

Then she hears a moan, but it is not her voice.

She gets up off the ground and walks towards the wooden crates, some smashed, and some still intact on top of the creature's body, who has now transformed back into Jonathan.

Laura terrifyingly looks on at the grisly site of bloody human remains and bones strewn all over the place on the warehouse floor from out of the busted wooden crates.

She then notices movement from underneath the crates as they begin to shift.

"He's still alive," she says to herself as she watches the crates begin to move, the next thing that happens completely takes Laura off guard as she watches in almost disbelief as one of the intact crates resting on top of Jonathan is propelled straight in the air and explodes, spewing carnage all over the warehouse floor.

"Shit!" she says to herself as she takes off running again towards a red door twenty-five yards down that had stood out to her also when she had entered the building with her romantic date turned killer.

"Fuck no!" she blurts out as she gets to the door and notices that it has a Biometric access reader installed on the wall next to it.

Then she gets an idea that might gain her entry, she quickly takes out a piece of paper and a lighter from her jacket and jams the paper underneath the door, setting it on fire! As the burning paper begin to produce smoke, Laura can now feel the presence of Jonathan closing in on her.

"Please, please, come on," she says to herself as she watches the paper that's almost burned out now when (Systems override) pops up in a neon red on the scanner.

The door makes a buzzing noise and then a resounding click, as Laura bursts thru the door quickly closing it behind her, she notices two security bolts on the door and engages them back into their locking position.

Laura turns around with the crowbar still in her hand, ready to bolt again, but comes to a dead freeze when her eyes begin to take in what is inside of the room with the red door.

With widened eyes and mouth agape, she looks on speechless at what looks like people, hundreds of them in rows, all ghastly pale and ghostly white lying on gurneys hook up to life support machines and intravenous lines that lead to large reservoir tubes filled with human -

Blood?

"Sonofabitch," Laura says to herself.

"So this is what you had in store for me."

Banggg! Banggg! Laura startled jumps away from the red door as something hits it so hard that it puts an indent in its structure.

Bang! The door concaves in; Laura looks on in fear knowing its just a matter of time before whatever it is behind it breaches the door.

"Fuck you asshole!" she says as she begins smashing the oversized tank like tubes, spilling their storage of human blood onto the floor.

An inhuman-like growl now comes from behind the door.

Bangggg! The door becomes unhinged and crashes to the floor, as Jonathan steps thru the opening with one thing on his mind, he's going to rip apart and devour this human being named Laura one piece at a time.

"Noooo! What have you done?" he screams out a Laura as he sees all of his hard labor and works spilled out on the floor.

His mind and sensory perception are off the charts with the smell of blood in the air, fresh blood, wasted blood.

And now he is going to make sure she wished she never spill a single drop.

"No need to hide Laura, I can smell your fear, your human stench, it's just a matter of time before I find you before I consume you," he says as he walks past the gurney of bodies, some splashed with the off cast of blood from the destroyed reservoirs.

Jonathan sniffs the air again, "Just a matter of time my little evasive friend before I find you, (he repeats) before I consume you."

"Consume this motherfucker!" Laura says as she springs up off one of the gurneys covered in blood and drives the crowbar deep into Jonathan's chest.

He stares into her eyes with those penetrating red pupils that now stars to fade as he grabs hold of the crowbar trying to pull the hot metal out of his chest.

Laura counteracts by driving the metal bar in deeper until she hears the crunch of bone and cartilage.

Jonathan collapses to the ground, and begin to cough up blood.

"Cock tease," he says with a wicked smile on his face.

"I've heard that before," Laura says unfazed.

"What a fucking mess you've made human," he says as he struggles to breathe, his pupils now turning a ghastly grey color.

"Can I ask you a question?"

"Yeah sure," Laura responds.

"How in the hell did you manage to topple those wooden crates like that?"

"I did what I had to do, I guess."

"There's been something that I've been trying to tell you all night Jonathan," Laura said.

"And what's that?"

"I identify as a woman, but I was born a man genetically."

"And why should that matter to me now human?"

"Because every relationship should begin and end with honesty," Laura said, a tear rolling down her bloody cheek.

"Laura."

"What?"

"I have a confession of my own."

"And what is that?"

"I am a vampire."

"I know."

THE END

CAMP FIREFLY

ORIGINAL STORY: BY LEE J. MINTER

ARTWORK BY: LEE J. MINTER

CHAPTER ONE

Entomophobia (also known as insectophobia) is a specific phobia characterized by an excessive fear of one or more classes of insect and classified as a phobia by the DSM-5
Source: **Wikipedia**

Petoskey Michigan, Camp Firefly, 1987.

A warm, humid breeze blows over Wallon lake as millions of stars illuminate its nighttime sky. The sound of insects and nocturnal little creatures big and small also fill the air as they search and forage for food in the burrows and crevices of its dense woods.

It is a typical night like all other nights at this soon to be open summer camp and getaway for children and young adults on summer break.

A typical night with one exception.

The blueish green meteoroid that cracks thru the night's atmosphere at more than *eight thousand miles an hour* the size of a Chevrolet Pacer plummeting towards the earth's surface, only miles away from the campsite.

The meteoroid now becomes a meteorite as it hits the ground with a loud explosion, decimating every living creature within a one-mile radius of its landing, creating a large burning crater in the ground.

The large anomaly now begins to sink into the cavity, as it turns the ground into mush underneath its weight. Blueish-green rays of light now shoot off the hissing rock like strobe lights illuminating the Petoskey woods sky miles away.

A group of men suddenly appear out of the woods in head to toe contamination suits with radioactive devices, as they slowly approach the alien rock.

“Get this cleanup gentleman as if it was never here,” orders the oic of the group.

“Sir shouldn’t this whole area be quarantine off, and this area be declared a biohazard zone until we find out what we are dealing with here?” one of his men ask.

The commander looks down on the ground and kicks a dead rabbit out of the way.

“Our orders as I stated is to get this shit cleanup and ally hoop out of here like we were never here before,” he barked.

“Any more questions?” he asked annoyed.

“Sir with all due respect that doesn't sound like proper protocol?” The same team member said.

The commander unholsters his forty-five semi-automatic pistol and fires one round close range into the head of his inquisitive team member; the bullet penetrates his subordinates face mask, shattering it in blood before he drops dead to the ground.

The other team members look on in shock.

He shines a flashlight on the ground, bends down and picks up his shell casing.

“Is that protocol enough for you,” he says bluntly.

The commander looks over his remaining crew.

“Any more damn questions?”

“No sir,” responds his second in command.

Chapter Two

Southfield Michigan, home to Jordan B. Cunningham, 1987

It was the biggest one that Jordan had seen yet slithering on the basement wall with what looks like a million tiny little legs all moving in a creepy cadence with each other. Oh' how he hated going down to the basement to retrieve anything that his mom "Deanna" may request at any given moment, all the wrong moments as far as he was concerned when he was at home.

Because Jordan forebodingly knew he was most likely at any given moment bound to run into any one of the many creepy crawlers that inhabited the dark and sometimes damp sanctuary of his family's basement. Spiders, Millipedes and Water Bugs that look like overgrown cockroaches.

And to him, the millipedes were the worst of the worst!

He stood there now in an almost catatonic state staring at the hideous creature with what looks like to him a thousand legs attached to its wormy body.

Aaaaaaahhh! Deanna his mother was the first one to hear the scream coming from the basement as she stood in the kitchen drying off dishes. Startled by the scream the plate she was drying slips out of her hand and goes crashing to her kitchen floor exploding in pieces.

Their little Pomsky dog, "Boo" reacted as well and started going nuts, spinning in circles and yapping at the top of his lungs.

"Shit!" what now? I swear that child is going to be the death of me," she said as she grabbed a can of bug spray out of the kitchen cabinet and prepared to head down to the basement.

Her older son Michael Jr. came running down the stairs from his bedroom to see what all the commotion was.

"What's wrong with butterfly now?" he asks his mom as he bit into the sandwich in his hand.

"Boy, did I not ask you to stop calling your brother by that name?" his mother reprimanded him.

"Sweep this broken plate off the floor before Boo, or someone cut their foot, while I go and see what got your brother so riled up."

"Probably an itsy bitsy spider," Michael said, making fun of his brother.

His mom shook her head sideways and proceeded down the basement stairs followed by their pomsky, Boo.

"Peanut I don't hear no broom," his mom yelled back upstairs.

"Mom I am getting to it, and pleaseeee stop calling me by my baby name," Michael whined.

"Jordan are you okay?" she shouted out! as she hurried down the basement stairs to the aid of her youngest son.

She quickly spotted Jordan standing in front of the basement wall in a frozen position. Her eyes went to the wall to see what had Jordan's undivided attention.

It was a large millipede or what she likes to call a legger that was making its way down the wall to less conspicuous quarters.

A large puff of spray hit the bug stopping it dead in its track; it slowly loosens its suction cup-like grip on the wall as it begins to curl up before it drops off the wall to its poisonous death on the floor.

"Jordan snap out of it, what's wrong with you?" Deanna said as she grabbed her eleven-year-old son by the arm.

He slowly begins to come out of his catatonic state. He was not even aware that a scream had left his mouth at this point.

"Big, big, bug," he stuttered.

"Jordan its just a harmless millipede and a dead one at that," his mom said, pointing at the now curled up millipede that did not seem so big after all.

"Dead?" Jordan said.

"Yes dead," his mom reassured him.

"Good, punk bug!" Jordan said.

"Yep, punk bug," his mom repeated, now wondering if she had made the right decision to send Jordan to Camp Firefly, despite his therapist assuring her that it was just this kind of activity that would assist Jordan in his development and coping with his insectophobia.

"Did you get what I asked you for down here?"

"My backpack and rain gear Mom?" he said.

"Yes," she replied.

Jordan held up his gear reluctantly.

"But I don't want to go, Mom," he said.

"Look Jordan we've already discussed this, and besides some fresh air and outdoor recreational activities is just what the doctor ordered."

"Well that doctor doesn't know shit!" he blurted out.

"Boy I am going to make you wash your mouth out with soap, now get up there and get ready to go, before we are late for camp," his mom said, tapping him on the butt.

Jordan took off running up the basement stairs to the sanctuary; he was more than glad to get out of the basement of creepy crawlers hidden in the dark just waiting to jump on him.

"Butterfly Bobby" is going to camp, butterfly don't let the bedbugs bite," his older brother Michael shouted out! as he watched his little brother bolt out of the basement door.

"Shut up peanut!" Jordan shouted back.

"What? I am going to get you, you little shit!" Michael said as he dropped the broom, to pursue his brother.

"Ouch!" he blurted out! jolted from the sting of a hand across the back of his neck. "Boy didn't I tell you to clean this mess up?" his mom said, now standing right beside him.

"He called me peanut," Michael protested.

"You've called him worst, now clean up this mess so that we can drop your little brother off at camp."

"Aw, Mom do I have to go, I promise to meet my boys at the park today."

'Your boys can wait," his mom said not persuaded.

"Jordan let's go!" she yelled upstairs to him.

"Mom I am coming," he shouted back downstairs un-enthusiastically.

Deanna watched as her son Jordan appear at the upstairs landing, of the stairwell, dragging his backpack slowly behind him.

"Jordan we are going to be late," she reiterated to him as she grabs him by the arm.

He slung the backpack strap around his other arm, sitting the backpack onto his back and small shoulders into an upright position.

"Let's go slug," his big brother Michael said with a grin on his face as he attempts to ruffle Jordan's hair only to get his hand slap away quickly by his younger brother.

"Cut it out you two, I don't need this horse shit right now!" their Mom said, as they all got into the station wagon.

"That's right it'll be plenty of it when you get to Camp Firefly, Jordan," Michael teased.

"It will probably smell better than your halitosis breath," Jordan said.

"Jordan that's not nice do you know that's a condition that thousands of people suffer from?" his mom interjected.

"I do now," Jordan answer.

"Hey Michael you are not alone," he added.

His brother turned around smirked and gave Jordan the finger.

Jordan looked back at his big brother with a smile of victory on his face as he continued playing a game of Donkey Kong on his Nintendo Game & Watch.

As Deanna headed north on Telegraph road, she was now only fifteen minutes away from the drop off point - Southfield Recreation Center where all the young adults and children that had signed up for the summer camp program would soon board a bus that would transport them up to Camp Firefly in Petoskey Michigan.

The recreational center parking lot was already full with the bustling activity of cars, children and their parents as Jordan 's mom pulled into the parking lot searching for a place to park.

Jordan was silently hoping that his mom did not find a parking space, that way she would not be able to go into the recreational center and send him off to his final demise.

Shit! No such luck, he thought, as he watched her pull into an empty parking space between two cars.

"I have to sign your brother off, I'll be right back," Deanna said to Michael, as she unbuckles her seatbelt.

Michel turns around in his seat to face Jordan "I am going to miss you, you little nerd," he said.

"Me too big nerd," Jordan said.

He tossed his brother the Nintendo Game & Watch. "Beat this score," he said.

"No shit!" Michael said as he looked down at the high score on the handheld video game.

The truth was, he liked his little brother, hell no, he loved him. He just had a funny way of showing it by teasing and goading him all the time. Michael watched thru the rearview mirror as his mom open the trunk to the station wagon and gather up all of his brothers camp gear.

The sound of the trunk closing reverberated thru the morning air.

Michael rolled down his car window, “Have fun at summer camp butterfly,” he shouted out to his brother.

Jordan turned around and gave him two middle fingers.

Michael snickered, as his eyes went over to a MILF dropping her children off at the recreational center also.

Chapter Three

"Butterfly," Jordan hated being called that, almost as much as he hated how he had earned that nickname.

His phobia with insects started according to his mom when he was just four years old when a butterfly landed on his forehead; she just happens to understandably so, leave out one important aspect of the event that his brother Michael was more than happy to fill in.

The embarrassing fact that he had peed all over himself while crying like a little girl, according to his sadist brother who swore that was the second funniest thing that he had ever seen in his fifteen years of smelly socks and dookey drawers on earth.

The fact that his older brother Michael also had not missed a window of opportunity to tease and goad him about that up to this day. Hence, the nickname Butterfly Bobby was born. Jordan remembers getting so mad at the teasing from his brother that one day he told his brother that his breath smell like old pootenanny.

When his mother found out what he had said, she asked him what he thought an old pootenanny was. His only answer was, "I came by Grandma's panties on the bathroom floor, and that's the best description I can give." He recalls in his memory how his mom couldn't stop laughing, but at the time he did not know why? Jordan smiles at this reflection, as he looks out the bus window at the passing landscape flying by as the bus makes it way up north.

Another passenger, a young man around his age, had fallen asleep with his Walkmans headphones on with his head resting on Jordan's shoulder. Jordan lifted the young man's head off his shoulder getting the sticky curl activator from his co-passengers Jheri-curl on the palm of his hand.

"Yuck," Jordan said as he wiped the sticky substance on the back of the seat in front of him.

"My bag," the young man said to Jordan as he begins to wake up, yawning, and outstretching his arms, almost hitting Jordan in the face.

Jordan pushed his arm down from out of the front of his face.

"Sorry bro, I was sleepy as fuckkkk, what's your name"? he asked as he put his headphones down over his neck.

Jordan looked at him apprehensively before responding. "Jordan," he answered.

"Jordan, I like that. My friends call me Juice," he said, offering Jordan a handshake.

Jordan shook a hand that was just as sticky as his hair.

"Show you right, " Juice responded, snapping his fingers.

Jordan looked at the other kid's glistening curls with specks of what looks like white lotion in his hair. He talked funny, and his hair was way too wet. Yeah, juice fitted him he guessed, but other than that he seemed cool.

"Nice to meet you juice," Jordan said.

"Don't say that until you get to know me," Juice said.

"Oh," Jordan said as he looked away nervously.

"I am just fucking with you homeboy," Juice said as he brushed up against Jordan's shoulder.

"Loosen up."

Jordan watched outside the window as the bus finally pulled into the Campgrounds, he had to admit the surroundings seemed nice as well as the buildings.

"Okay Campers we are here," the bus driver announce as the bus came to a squealing halt.

"Everyone, please make sure you get your bags and property from the overhead compartments, and luggage, when you get off the bus, and I hope you all enjoy your stay at Camp Firefly."

"I will if there are some fly girls around," Juice said with a grin, as he elbows Jordan.

Jordan had to wait until Juice got his stuff out of the overhead compartment and the bus aisle cleared before he was able to start making his way off the bus.

He noticed the Camp Counselors and assistants starting to divide the children up by age groups as they exited the bus.

"All children 5-8 report over here, to the red group, 9-13 the yellow group and anyone older than thirteen the green group," announce the "young brunette" camp assistant Bethenny Jones on the bullhorn.

"Welcome everyone to your seven-day adventure here at Camp Firefly, if there is anything you need, please let any assistant, counselor or advocate know, and we will do our best to accommodate you," she said with a smile.

"Sounds good to me," Juice leans into Jordan and whispered.

"With that being said campers, please give a warm welcome to our Camp Director Jamie Flowers."

The crowd of kids and teens led by the counselors begin applauding and chanting the Director's first name.

"Jamie, Jamie, Jamie."

"Man she must look like a porn star with a name like that," Juice said to Jordan.

A middle-aged man, balding, with round glasses, banana shorts and striped tube socks walked up to a podium with a microphone positioned in front of the camp attendees.

"There is your porn star," Jordan said, barely able to hold in his laughter.

Juice look on slightly embarrassed.

The Camp Director fidgeted with his mic for a second as he looks upon his waiting audience.

"All I have to say is welcomeee to Camp Fireflyyyy!" he said, met by a raucous applaud.

Mr. Flowers then waited until his audience had calmed down.

"Now hit it !" he said, as a song from Kool and the Gang kicked in on the loudspeakers on each side of him. "Celebrate good times come on," the lyrics blared from the speakers.

"Man my momma think that's the shit!" Juice said as he begins dancing to the song.

"Man you're crazy, and I am tired," Jordan said, picking up his duffle bag off the nicely manicured grass.

"Homeboy don't be an L'seven the party's just started at Camp Fireflyyy," Juice said, mocking the director.

"Whatever," Jordan said annoyed.

"Group yellow," please allow me to show you to your accommodations and get you guys all settled in," Bethenny said.

"She can settle me in anytime if you know what I mean?" Juice said, to Jordan winking his eye.

"Her or Flowers?" Jordan said.

"Man, don't play me for no fool," Juice said curtly.

"My bag," Jordan apologize.

"I do sweet & juicy, not sweet and low," Juice said, patting one side of his curls while lugging his bags.

"Word up," Jordan said.

Jordan looked back at Juice confused.

"Juice what's sweet & low?" he asked.

Juice laughed.

"Man you're an L seven," Juice replied.

"No, I am not!" Jordan shot back defensively.

The Camp assistant turned around to address both boys.

"Campers, please pay attention to my instructions while I am escorting you to your Cabin," she said.

"Yes Ms. Jones," Juice said.

Juice batted his eyes and broke into a discreet campy impersonation of the Camp assistant. "Campers, please pay attention to my instructions while I am escorting you to your cabin," he said softly.

Jordan laughed, but this time he elbows Juice.

When they arrived at their assigned cabin, number two, Jordan noticed it was fairly spacious inside with eight beds, four across on each side of the room, with footlockers next to them.

"I got dibs on this bed," Juice said as he went over and sat his stuff down on one of the beds.

"Okay guy's I know it's been a long bus ride in, and I am sure, everyone is starving, so get settle in, put your things away, and I'll come back to escort you over to Cedar Hall for dinner at 4:00 pm," Bethenny said.

"Kumbaya," shouted out one of the campers, a chubby kid that was big for his age, causing everyone in the group to burst out in laughter.

"Kumbaya," repeated Bethenny with a smile.

"4:00 pm troopers," she reminded everyone again, before exiting the cabin.

"Troopers how old do she think we are five?" Juice said quietly to Jordan, his new found friend.

When she was out of sight, he walked over to Ben, and high five him.

" Kumbaya homeboy that shit was funny, what's your name?"

"Barry."

"Man you built like "the fridge," Juice said observantly.

"I guess," the big kid said shrugging as if he was slightly uncomfortable with his size.

"Barry I am Juice, and this is my homeboy Jordan across from me."

"Word," Barry said sizing them both up.

Jordan nodded his head in acknowledgment and began taking personal items out of his bags and placing them in his footlocker next to his bed.

"Man, look at him Barry, this dude doesn't waste any time," Juice said grinning.

Jordan looked back up at Juice slightly annoyed.

"Well I guess I might as well start unpacking my shit to homey," he said.

Juice begins to unpack his bag as well when something he pulls out catches Jordan's eye.

"Man, what the hell are those?" he asks Juice.

"What these?" Juice says as he holds up his leopard printed underwear.

"Yeah those," Jordan confirmed.

"The latest in men's underwear bee," he answered.

"Those look like my Grandma panties," Jordan said.

Barry smiled and snickered.

"If they do, I would love to meet your Grandma," Juice said.

"Sure, and you can give her back her panties," Jordan retorted.

Barry burst out laughing. "Good one bee."

"Clam it, fat boy!" Juice said as he gave Barry a dirty look.

And although Barry was much larger that tone and look on Juice's face told him that Juice was no one to underestimate.

"I am not fat, just big boned," Barry said in his defense.

Still, despite his reservations, he shot back Juice a mean glare, which wasn't lost on Juice.

Juice knew he could probably take Jordan, but the big one Barry would be a whole different story, and he didn't come to summer camp to get his ass whoop on the first day here, so to save face, he felt it was best to keep his cool.

"It's all good ass wipes, yall momma still buying yall draws," Juice said, and gave them both the finger.

"And my momma buys my little sister draws like that too," Barry said.

Jordan burst out laughing; It appeared that the big kid had a sense of humor, maybe he wasn't so bad after all he thought.

"Ha ha ha, two freaking comedians," Juice said as he threw the underwear in his footlocker angrily.

Jordan suddenly started to feel bad about them teasing Juice; he knew how it was to be teased, to be bullied.

"Juice it's all good we are just messing with you bro," he said extending his hand in friendship.

Juice looked at Jordan's hand and then waited a few seconds before he shook it.

Barry walked over, and Juice did the same.

From here on out or at least for seven days he knew these two would be his cool camp brothers, now where in the hell he thought, did he put his soft n sheen no drip curl activator.

Chapter Four

It was now day three at Camp Firefly, days filled with various activities for the camp goers like hiking, campfires, and horseback riding.

And for the more adventurous, kayaking, zip lining, and rock climbing, preceded of course, by more campfires.

Day three in the Camp's Nature Center Entomologist and guest speaker Peter Doogen held the attention span of young and older campers in a classroom, as he gave a vivid show and tell lecture on the various species of insects that inhabited Camp Firefly and planet earth.

All of the attendees seem impressed and interested, in what Dr. Doogen had to say. All of them except Jordan, (that is) who was starting to feel ill. He could feel Juice's eye's on him, how in the hell he thought had he allowed this nitwit to talk him into attending this event, attending his phobia?

He had tried everything possible to talk himself out of attending this thing without drawing suspicion to himself to no avail.

But he knew he could not allow his two new friends to know that he was scared of bugs either, what would they think of him he wonders if they found out?

The last thing he wanted was them to think was he was a puss, a scary cat or uncool to be around.

"Jordan are you okay?" Juice asks.

"Yeah it must be something I ate for breakfast," Jordan said looking noticeably queasy.

"You don't look too good dude," Barry said, sitting at a desk across from Jordan.

How did he let these two talk him into this? Jordan thought again.

Juice: "Hey man wouldn't it be cool to see one of the largest cockroaches on earth?"

Jordan: "No."

Barry: "how large?"

Juice: "I heard at least 3.1 inches."

Barry: cool.

Jordan: "Sounds disgusting."

Barry: "I heard Dr. Doolittle got some mad insects."

Juice: "You in or what homey?"

Barry: "Hey Jordan's not faded by any bugs, right 'J'?"

Jordan: "Of course not."

Juice: "Then let's bounce and see some weird ass bugs campers."

It all now came back to Jordan, that's how he had ended up here sitting in a classroom full of the creepy crawling, and slimy monsters that he had feared all his life.

He watched intently as Peter Doogen made his way down the aisle of the classroom, showing off the various insects or bugs that he had discussed earlier to a captive audience of his fellow campers.

Jordan watched as Doogen was now only a few feet away from him with a small aquarium in his hand.

"Man that's one big ass roach!" his friend Juice said.

And that's all Jordan would remember right before he passed out.

"Jordan, Jordan, are you okay?" he heard a voice say as he was slowly coming to, but the faces that were looking at him was still a blur as he attempted to focus.

The camp nurse stood over him staring down into his face.

"Yeah I am okay," he said, his head hurt slightly, and his neck was slightly stiff but other than that he felt okay.

He sat upright in the bed and looked around; he was in the Camp's infirmary.

"Man we thought you were a ghost," Juice said.

"Naw I am straight," Jordan said trying to put on a tough front on for his two friends.

"Man your eyes roll back into your head before you pass out; I thought you were turning into a zombie dude," Barry said, as he then proceeded to give Jordan a brief demonstration by shaking and rolling his eyes back in his head.

"Man you illin bee," Juice said.

"Okay boys give your friend some time to rest, and he will join you later," the nurse said as she hands Jordan a glass of water.

"All your vitals check out Jordan, and we contacted your Mom to see if you had a history of seizures or passing out?" the pretty nurse said.

Jordan shook his head back no, as he passes her back the water.

"A camp counselor will be in here to talk to you shortly," she said.

Jordan looked at the nurse nervously as he already pictured in his mind what the Camp Counselor was going to say, "Why were you in a room full of bugs when you have Insectophobia? This summer program is a step by step process, not jumping out of a plane without a parachute process Mr. Cunningham."

But there were fucking bugs everywhere, and he knew it, especially outside.

After a phone call to his mom to confirm that he was okay and that he had decided to stay for the remaining four days, Jordan exited the infirmary at least with the fact that the staff had not divulged the real reason to his compadre's why he had fainted in class.

He knew now that he just had to figure out a better way to cope with his problem, after all, he knew in reality that he was bigger than the things that he feared the most.

"Fuck Butterfly Bobby," he whispers under his breath to himself, as he picked up a rock off the ground and hurled it at a nearby tree.

The daylight suddenly begins to darken as a raindrop hit his face, Jordan wiped the raindrop off his cheek, which was soon follow by more raindrops and the crackling sound of thunder.

"Shit!" he blurted out.

A voice suddenly came over the camp's loudspeakers mounted on its buildings. "*All campers this a weather alert for your safety, please return to your assigned cabins, all campers please return to your assigned cabins or facilities until further notice*!"

"*All campers this is a weather alert for your safety, please...*"

Jordan took off running to his cabin *# 2* underneath what had now become a torrential downpour of rain and thunder

When he finally made to the cabin, he was soaking wet.

As he entered the cabin, he noticed that some of his fellow lodgers were watching the show ALF on a television mounted above on a bracket.

The Alien puppets voice resonated thru out the room.

"Hey man you look like a wet possum," a familiar voice said, laughing.

"Thanks," Jordan said as he went over to his area of the room and began removing his wet clothes before changing into some dry ones.

"Looks like it's going to be "pizza night," Barry said, looking out at the downpour of rain beating against the cabin roof.

"Pizza sweetttt!" one of the other young campers in the room shouted out that happen to hear within earshot what Barry had said about tonight's dinner.

"Nerd heaven," Juice said, as he looked over at the other camper.

"Proudly, but at least my pillow cases stay dry juicehead," the other camper countered.

"What was that nerd?" Juice said angrily.

"Man chill," Jordan said.

"I know why you like pizza it reminds you of your face," Juice said.

The kid looked up from his bunk and gave Juice the finger.

"Man if I was back in the hood I'll beat the stink off that boy," Juice said feeling disrespected.

"I did not know Farmington Hills was the hood?" Barry said.

"It's not," Jordan answer, giving Juice a "are you for real look" seeing right thru his bullshit as he slips on a dry camp firefly t-shirt.

"Whatever," Juice said.

"How are you feeling bee?" Barry ask.

"Well I could have spent more time with that nurse," Jordan said.

"Word, that nurse was bodacious," Juice said grinning.

"A Brickhouse," Barry concurred.

"Hey, guy's turn that shit down!" Juice scream at the other campers watching the television.

"Who watches tv anyway during summer camp but nerds," he added.

"Hey guy's pizza delivery," Bethenny said as she came thru the door carrying several large box pizzas covered in a bag, another camp assistant accompanied her with a rolling cooler filled with water, soft drinks, and a bag filled with paper plates and eating utensils.

The campers joined her over at a picnic table that was one of two in the middle of the floor of the cabin.

Another camp assistant entered the cabin shortly afterward with more food (Salad) in a rolling container.

"Hey Bethenny," Juice said leering at the attractive camp counselor that was at least four years his senior.

"Hi Franklin," she said.

"Franklin?" Jordan and Barry both blurted out at the same time, bursting in laughter.

"Laugh on clowns," Juice said.

"She is just coy, but once she have some of the juice, she ain't going to want to have milk," he boasted, rubbing his chin.

"Boy, you couldn't tap that if you had a million dollars in your pocket," Barry said discreetly.

"I don't need a million dollars because unlike you I got game scrubs," Juice said.

Bethenny looked over towards them and smiled, Juice wink at her and smile back patting his hair.

"Franklin do you have something in your eye?" she asked.

"No ma'am," he answers embarrassed.

Jordan and Barry burst out laughing again.

"Assholes," Juice said underneath his breath.

Juice felt a set of eyes on him; it was the kid with the braces on his teeth that he had insulted earlier, smiling at him while he ate his pizza.

He gave the kid back the evilest stare he could muster up, but it did not deter the kid from staring.

"Creepy fucker," he said to himself as he got a plate of pizza.

Chapter Five

The rain and thunder did not let up until much later that night after all the campers had retired for tonight.

The cabin smelled like ass and feet to Jordan, and all he could hear was snoring throughout the cabin as he tosses and turns to get to sleep, in his bed.

And that's when he heard an unfamiliar sound, like something moving, now slithering on the wooden cabin floor. He sheepishly looked above his covers but did not see anything.

Shoo, shu, shu, shu shu, shu, was the sound. "Hey Juice are you awake?" he said quietly to his neighbor. But all he could hear from his buddy Juice was loud snoring, and the occasional crunching of the plastic cap Juice wore on his head to keep his Jheri-curls moisturize.

Shoo, shu, shu, shu, shu, shu.

"Hey is anyone there?" he asks softly, still afraid to look above his footboard.

Shoo, shu, shu, shu, shu, shu.

Silence.

Whatever it was sound like something with many legs all moving in synchronicity with each other, and Jordan only knew one thing that sounds like that! He finally psychs up enough nerve to sit up in his bed and look above the bed footboard while still clinging to his sheets.

He could hear the rain starting back again accompanied by the crackling of lighting then thunder.

A bluish color light flashed in the few cabin windows when the sound of thunder erupted again.

Jordan slowly eases up in his bed, gripping his sheets and blankets so tight his palms hurt.

His mouth fell open, but a scream never came out of it, as he watches the gigantic millipede quickly slither its way towards Juice's bed.

The twelve-foot long giant insect slithers his way up onto his friend's bed and grabs Juice by his head as his plastic shower cap falls off and begins dragging Juice's body out of his bed, across the wooden floor, out of the cabin.

"Juice, juice, juice…" Jordan wants to cry out his friend's name, but nothing comes out of his mouth, nothing.

Jordan watches as Juice's feet with tube socks on them is the last part of his body to disappear out of the cabin door.

The sound of thunder cracks the night air again sending cold chills thru Jordan's body causing him to shiver as he looks on in a trance-like state.

His gaze never leaves the cabin door that's open letting the rain in, letting whatever's outside. The first thing he sees is the reciprocating antennae of the large insect coming thru the door.

As the insectoid slowly enters he can vaguely make out what it is. It is not until it gets closer that he sees that is an abnormally large cockroach, almost the size of a man quickly skittering across the wooden floor towards his scent. Jordan goes underneath his sheets as he feels the mutation pass him by, he catches the sound of its wings fluttering on its oily back as if it's about to take flight.

Silence.

Then the screams of one of his fellow campers, brings him back to his nightmare, followed by the sounds of the ripping and tearing of flesh by those scissor-like jaws of the monster in his cabin.

The sound of something metal drops on the floor next to his bed.

Jordan peeks out with one eye above his sheet and retrieves the small flashlight that he sleeps with from underneath his pillow. He shines the flashlight on the floor next to his bed only to see it's a pair of metal dental braces with gums and blood on them on the floor.

A musty smell permeates Jordan's nostrils.

Clickety, clickety, click…

Clickety, clickety..

Click.

An audible scream erupts from Jordan's mouth as his flashlight illuminates the large Blattodea (cockroach) crawling up on his bed for another meal.

His flashlight falls to the floor and goes dim.

Barry awakes out of his sleep to what sounds to him like the buzzing of a loud fire alarm.

He gets up out of his bed, stepping into something slimy and wet on the floor.

Must be leftover pizza he thinks, as he lumbers over to the wall and flips the light switch on to the inside of the cabin.

When the light comes on, he immediately freezes in a state of horror and shock as he now watches all the various species of giant bugs wrecking havoc on his fellow campers in a blood-splattered frenzy of insectoid mayhem.

Bizzzzz… bizzzzz… bizzzzzz.

Barry looks around in the air confused, but unfortunately, he does not see the raptor sized mosquito behind him honing in on its target "him."

Barry instantly feels a sharp stab of pain in his neck, as the mosquito's proboscis penetrates his flesh like an oversize razor-sharp needle ripping thru tendons and muscle.

The boy struggles but only for a moment as the insect drives its needle-like nose in deeper, its abnormal weight and size bringing Barry to his knees as he feels the blood being suck from his body.

The raptor sized mosquito removes his needle-like proboscis from the back of Barry's neck, as Barry struggles to get up, and quickly plunges it into the back of the boy's head paralyzing his prey to the floor like a thumbtack on a paper memo, as it returns to feeding amongst the carnage.

• • •

Jordan is jolted from his sleep by the nightmare as he springs into a sitting position in his bed. He is hyperventilating and struggles to catch his breath as he looks around the cabin to see if his fellow campers are still alive, and not torn apart by the monstrous insects in his dream.

He can see that most of them are still sound to sleep, and none of them was dissected and torn apart by monstrous insects like in his dream.

Jordan slowly begins to breath normal again as his heartbeat slows down. He looks over at the bed next to him, where Juice is sleeping, but all he sees is a shower cap on the pillow of Juices bed.

"Juice?" he shouts out loud as he gets out of his bed, to look for his friend.

"Barry wake up, Juice is missing!" he says, shaking his other friend awake.

"No, he's not he went to the bathhouse," Barry says groggily, holding his pillow tight.

Jordan looks over at Juice's bed again, and sure enough, his shower slippers are missing.

"The bathhouse?" Jordan said, as if still not convinced.

"Yeah, what are you his mother?" Barry said, annoyed because Jordan had awakened him and all he wanted to do was get back to sleep.

"I know we homeboys but damn you two don't see enough of each other?" Juice said, coming thru the door in his bathrobe while drying off his wet hair with the towel he held in his hands.

"I saw your plastic cap on the bed, and I thought…" Jordan said stopping in mid-sentence.

"You thought what homey?" Juice said still grinning.

"Nevermind," Jordan said.

"He thought something had happened to you?" Barry groaned, with the pillow still over his head.

"Nope, Juice is still Juice," their friend said patting his body down.

"Yo homeboys do you guys wanna go get some breakfast or not?" Juice asks.

"Sure," Jordan said.

"Barry gets your lazy ass up, and let's go homie," Juice said tugging on Barry's pillow.

"Fuck you," Barry said.

"That's cool it's not like your fat ass can't afford to miss a meal or a hundred," Juice stated.

" Jordan is that pancakes and bacon I smell?" Juice said sniffing the air.

"Smell like it," Jordan agreed.

"I smell'em too, hold up guy's I am getting up now," Barry said.

Juice laughed.

"You dudes know what today is?" Jordan said excitedly.

"No," Jordan said as he tied his gym shoes.

"Man you gotta be joking? Today is the day we get to see flamethrowers in action.

"Oh yeah, the flamethrower event," Barry said as he put on his camp t-shirt.

"How exciting a pyromaniac's wet dream," Jordan said not impressed.

"A pyro what? Homie you trippin we gotta go," Juice said.

"By the way 'J' what is a Pyromaniac?"

Jordan looked at Juice was he serious, he thought, then he remembers it was Juice.

Barry shook his head sideways grinning.

"I'll explain it to you later dude on the way to breakfast," he answered.

"Seriously man, you don't know what a Pyro is? You need to get yourself a dictionary bee," Barry teased.

"I don't have to your mama will teach me when your daddy's not home," Juice joked.

Barry gave juice the middle finger.

CHAPTER SIX

The flamethrower event was not only designed to teach the young campers about fire safety but also the hazard of playing and being careless with fire when out camping and at home, and of course a short lecture on the history of flamethrowers and their various uses.

Despite all this, the flamethrowers were still no doubt the main attraction of the event and any one of the kids would have loved to have what look like a badass *Super Soaker* that shot flames fifty-feet or more instead of water in their possession.

The local fireman from the Petoskey Fire Department was there also with an engine on hand just in case things with awry.

"Man that's fresh," Juice said as he looks on at the instructors shooting streams of flames in the air, one stream appears to go at least seventy-five feet or more.

"Can we get one volunteer up here?" said one of the Instructors that had a flamethrower with two cylinder tanks already attached to it, unlike the other ones carried by two more instructors that required you to carry a backpack of three-cylinder tanks.

All the campers raised their hands, amongst shouts of "Me, me, me!"

"You young man step right on up," the instructor said as he pointed to Jordan.

Jordan looked back at the instructor wearing what he thought was a ghostbuster jumpsuit rip off stunned by the invitation to participate.

"Me," the word barely came out of his mouth, as he pointed back at himself.

"Yes, you son step on up," insisted the instructor.

Juice and Barry patted Jordan on the back in support.

"Go ahead Jordan show them how it's done son," Juice shouted out.

Jordan steps out amongst his friends into the lion's den.

"Okay camper this is a smaller version of the flamethrower which has two cylinders one cylinder holds compressed gas, the other cylinder flammable liquid call petrol," the Instructor said, pointing at the cylinders as he describes them.

"What is your name son?"

"Jordan."

"Did you just understand what I just said?"

"One cylinder holds compressed air the other fuel," Jordan answered.

"Excellent smarty pants, now stand behind me, I am going to demonstrate how you fire off this thing, no pun intended, and then I am going to give you a shot at it okay."

"Excellent," Jordan said, causing the other campers to laugh.

"Now it's your turn Jordan," the Instructor said as he handed Jordan off the flamethrower and positioned it in his hands.

"You see that hornet's nest on that tree Jordan?"

"No."

"That's because the tree and the nest are imaginary Jordan," the instructor said, to laughing by their audience which made Jordan even more nervous.

"Okay," Jordan said timidly.

"Now at the count to five you are going to let loose on that annoying hornet's nest that's been plaguing your family's backyard, okay?"

"Okay."

"One, two, three, four, five."

Jordan tilted the flamethrower at an angle and decompressed the trigger on it shooting out a fifty-foot flame into the air at his imaginary hornet's nest in his imaginary tree to a round of applause to those in attendance.

"Good job Jordan, and another round of applause for this brave young man folks," the Instructor said.

"And please remember folks don't try this at home, drunk or stupid."

The campers all laughed again.

"We will have one more volunteer…" before the Instructor could finish his sentence the crack of thunder filled the air, and then it starts raining.

'Okay guy's I guess we are going to have to wrap it up, thanks for your participation and enjoy the rest of your summer camp," the Instructor said to the sounds of disappointment.

The rain hits harder now, as everybody starts scattering and running for shelter and cover.

"Get these throwers on the truck guy's so that we can get the hell out of this rain," says the Instructor that gave Jordan a personal lesson.

"Hey are you guy's staying for dinner?" Camp Director Jamie Flowers ask the boss of the crew.

"You bet Mr. Flowers we wouldn't miss that spaghetti and fish sticks for the world," he shouted back thru the rain, giving him a thumbs up.

"See you at Cedar Hall boys," Flowers said as he took off running towards the camp's dining facility.

"I think that dude's got a thing for flamethrowers," says one of his instructors.

"And yellow shorts," adds the boss, as they all laugh.

"Shit! what the fuck was that?" says one of the other instructors as he slaps at a mosquito on his arm that has just bitten him.

"Lets' get the fuck out of this rain, these mosquitos out here are vicious as fuck!" he said.

The instructor looks at the size of the bite and the amount of blood running down one of his instructor's arm.

"Dude that looks more like a snake bite to me you sure it was a mosquito?" he asks.

"Yeah I smash the little bugger right here," he says showing the palm of his hand.

"What the fuck?" his boss says as he looks at the palm of his guy's hand completely covered in blood and bug parts.

"That must have been one big ass mosquito."

The instructor looks at his hand, "Boss I think I am starting to feel sick," he says as he grabs his throat and begins wheezing before he passes out and collapses to the ground.

"What the hells wrong with him?" said one of the other workers.

"Hey dickheads don't just stand there he's sick, get him the fuck inside and out of the rain," ordered the boss.

Something flies in front of his face as he swats it with his baseball cap, knocking it to the ground, it lands with a splash in one of the rain puddles.

He walks over to look at it.

It's a mosquito the size of a Side-blotched Lizard 2.5 inches long, wings crumpled, lying in the puddle dying.

"Holy shit what the monkey splunk is that thing," he says pointing at the puddle with the strange but large crumple insect.

Chapter Seven

The supervisor of the flamethrower crew ordered one of his men to put the dying crumpled insect inside of a large empty jar, just in case the medical staff on hand at the camp wanted to know what kind of insect had bitten one of his instructors. It turns out to be a good afterthought on the supervisor's part that inevitably saves his co-workers life.

The camp's doctor had informed the supervisor that the man and co-worker that he referred to by the nickname "Reefer" had gone into an anaphylactic shock after being bitten by the mosquito and that he had administered him an epinephrine injection to counteract his allergic reaction to the bite.

He would be fine now and just needed some rest he also informed him.

"Shit doc it looks like me, and my boys are staying for tonight huh?"

"That would be wise so that we can monitor "Reefer's" I mean Mr. Smith's recovery until he's back on his feet."

"Man that's one big ass mosquito Dr. Ward," the flamethrowers supervisor said looking at the large bluish color insect that was now dead inside the jar sitting on the lab counter.

"Yes quite unusual for its size, the camp's resident doctor agreed.

"That's a fucking understatement!" a voice said that seem to come out of nowhere but soon enter the room, it was Peter Doogen, the Entomologist who had overheard their conversation, accompanied by Mr. yellow shorts himself, Camp Director Jamie Flowers.

"Dr. Doogen," how are you? Dr. Ward said dryly.

"Chipper Dr. Lard," he answered.

"Ward," Dr. Ward corrected.

"Yes, yes, Ward," Doogen said patting Dr. Ward on the arm.

He had long got the impression that Dr. Ward did not consider him a real doctor, and therefore he had no problem, showing Ward equal contempt for his lack of respect for his academic credentials.

Now was Dr. Doogen's time to shine, and he had no problem doing so either. He walked over to the jar with the dead mosquito inside and picked it up, raising the jar above his head as he turns it around in his hands inspecting the culprit that had almost cost a man his life.

"You are a big one aren't you fella?" he said.

"Too big actually," he said to everyone in the room as he sat the jar back down on the counter.

"What we have here is a super skeeter," he said.

"That sounds like a porno movie I've seen," the flamethrowers boss said with a grin.

"A different kind of skeeter I am sure," Doogen said eyebrow raised.

"No, the super skeeter is a "summer floodwater mosquito" usually a half-inch long, this baby is twice its size," Doogen pointed out.

"In fact, it is strangely compatible in size with the largest mosquito in the world which is the Toxorhynchites speciosus endemic to coastal regions of Australia."

"Pete, are you saying we got ourselves some kind of mutant mosquito?" Jamie said.

"Yes, and God knows what else out there?" Doogen said.

The flamethrower instructor looks at them baffled.

" Hey man this stuff is way too heavy for me, you guys don't mind if I grab myself some dinner before those greedy little bastards eat it all up do you?" he said.

"Those greedy little bastards are called campers," Jamie said.

"That's what I meant Mr. Flowers."

"Bon appetit."

The three of them watch the head flamethrower instructor leave the room, and when he was out of earshot, Jamie let loose.

" Shame, shame, shame, all beef, and no brains, I hope that idiot doesn't burn down his house one day," Jamie said tapping his finger on his cheek.

Doogen thought his comment was funny and laughed; Ward remained unfazed. He looks at the mosquito in the jar again; it was something about it that he did not notice before and that was it seems to have a weird blueish glow to it that almost illuminated the jar.

"Doogen, do you think we need to quarantine the children and staff until we find out what's going on?" Jamie wanted to know.

"Jamie that might be the best thing to do at least until I find out what the hell is going on here," Doogen said.

"I am going to take this mosquito and run some tests on it and get back with you," he said picking up the jar.

He looked over at Dr. Ward who had this weird expression on his face and then realizes it wasn't just the academic discourtesy that made the man repulsive to him; it was something else unsettling about him that he just couldn't put his finger on at this time.

"Are you okay, Dr. Ward?" he asked catching him off guard.

"Yes, I was just concern about the children's summer camp being interrupted by what may just be a pebble in the water," he said.

"A pebble that may turn out to be a boulder, if we are not careful Dr. Ward," Doogen countered.

"Yes, excuse the crude metaphor, but shit does roll downhill sometimes eh' Dr. Doogen," he replied with that underlying cynicism that made Peter want to plant a foot in his ass.

"And sometimes up Dr. Ward and sometimes up," Doogen rebuttal.

"I'll contact you Jamie with the lab results."

"Thank you, Peter, and have a safe drive back to Ann Arbor," Jamie said, shaking Doogen's hand.

"I wish you the same Dr. Doogen, and I'll be looking forward to those test results as well," Ward said.

Peter nodded his head at Dr. Ward as he departed, he had a long drive back to Ann Arbor, and it was getting dark.

When the room was empty, and Dr. Ward was sure that no one else was present he nervously made the phone call that he knew he was obligated to make.

He patiently listens to the ringing on the other side, before the other party finally picked up their line.

"Major Stone," a deep, gruff voice answer.

"Major Stone this is Dr. Ward, sir we might have a problem."

"Red Flag," the major said flatly.

"Red Flag," Dr. Ward repeated.

"E.T.A. two hours before *Operation Clean Sweep*," Major Stone said.

Chapter Eight

Jordan had no idea what was up with the weather only that it reminded him of the weather in his nightmare, rainy and stormy with flashes of blue light as he laid in his bed now awake, amongst the rest of his peers who were dead asleep in the cabin.

Jordan raised up and looked over at Juice who was snoring with his mouth open, reminding him of an old lady with that shower cap on his head to keep the moisture in his curls. Jordan shook his head sideways as he laid back down.

He looked over at one of the cabin windows and watched the flashes of blue light illuminate thru every time the sound of thunder erupted in the darkness of the room. A feeling of dread suddenly crept over him, what if the nightmare that he had recently was a warning and a sign of the things to come, he thought.

Jordan raised up and look over at his other friend Barry, he was fast asleep also, counting sheep Jordan thought.

That's it he thought, his mom always said if you have trouble sleeping count sheep. Jordan closes his eyes and begins counting in his mind "1, 2, 3, 4, 5, 6, 7, 8," his eyes flew open at eight. Okay, that didn't help he thought. He found that option more annoying than relaxing.

Jordan took the small flashlight he kept from underneath his pillow, leaned down over his bed and pulled out one of the bed drawers, and reached in and pulled out a Black Beat magazine and begin scanning thru the pages while shining the flashlight on the pages.

He found an interesting story on Grandmaster Flash and the Furious Five and begin reading the article, his eyes soon begin to get heavy midway thru the story, and the flashlight rolled from his hand onto the bed as he finally fell to sleep.

A loud crashing noise and the sound of screams and emergency horns whaling jolted Jordan out of his sleep as he sprung up in his bed eyes wide. And when he was able to focus his eyes, he realizes he was not the only one awake; all his fellow campers were sitting up in their beds too, all seven of them staring ahead, scared in the dark.

How long had he been asleep? He thought, an hour. His flashlight was still on as he picks it up off the bed.

"What the hell is going on out there Armageddon?" Juice said as he got out of the bed.

Screams from outside erupt again, causing most of the children to jump out of there skin as they slowly walk towards the cabin windows and the door.

Ringgggg, ringgggg, ringgggg, "Can someone get the phone," Juice said.

Jordan rushed over to the wall phone and picked it up, "Hello," he said feebly into the phone.

"Do not turn on the lights and barricade the doors we are under attack!" scream a distressed voice from the other end of the phone.

Jordan stood in terror by the sound of the voice and how he was able to get his next words out of his mouth was beyond his understanding, but he did.

"From what?" he asks.

They are coming! Oh no, they are here, oh no, aaaaaahhhhhhhh! Dead silence.

Jordan drops the receiver, "Do not turn on the lights and we need to barricade these doors, he said we are under attack!" Jordan barked out orders as his brain immediately went into fight mode.

"What the hell are you talking about bro, and who's he? Juice said.

"Man I am going out there to see what the hell is going?" Juice said standing by the door.

"Juice no!" Jordan screams out.

But it was too late; it happens so quick that no one was for sure what had happened or at least wanted to admit to what they thought they saw. But one thing was for sure something large, black, and worm-like snatched Juice up quickly by the head, in its mandibles as soon as he opened that door and dragged him swiftly off into the night kicking and screaming for his young life.

"Juiceeee!" Barry scream.

"Close that fucking door! " Jordan shouted out.

The other campers rushed to the door to close it and begin barricading the door from inside. The only thing that was a reminder that Juice had been standing only seconds ago in that doorway was his oily shower cap on the floor.

"Hey, Jordan check this shit out!" Barry said as he and a few of the other campers stood crammed up by the window trying to get a view of the mayhem outside.

Jordan made his way over to the window, pushing a few of the other campers out of the way so that he could get a better view. And what he was now looking at was even worse than his nightmare, it was as if the gates of hell had open themselves.

Giant mutant insects where flying everywhere, crashing into things and attacking people joined by other monstrosities of giant bugs of various species, that was ripping the camp and its people apart.

In the middle of this spectacle of mayhem and madness, Jordan noticed the crew of flamethrowers was barely holding their own, as they incinerated any flying or crawling anomaly that was stupid enough to get within one-hundred feet or less of their handheld cremators.

The sound of glass shattering across the room and screams whirls Jordan and Barry around.

"Shit!" Barry shouts out as he sees a giant mosquito on top of one of one his fellow campers about to drive its sword-like proboscis thru the other kid's skull.

The other kids quickly grab their gym shoes and begin beating the giant mosquito on top of the boy to a bloody pulp, as it makes a loud buzzing noise thrashing back and forward.

Barry screams and comes down on the mutant insects head with a bedpost; its head explodes into a pulp splattering its brain matter all over its combatants.

"Yuk!" says one of the combatants, as it splashes on his face and glasses.

Barry kicks the headless mosquito off his fellow camper, who is in shock but unfortunately unhurt and helps him off the floor.

Jordan looks on in horror and then looks down at the bloody gym shoe in his trembling hand and smiles. He did not freeze this time he thinks; he realizes he has fought back at something much bigger than he has ever seen in his life and this time he was not scared.

"Man, why don't you have any bug juice on your shoe?" Barry asks a camper holding red and white gym shoes that still looks new and unscathed.

"Man these are those new Michael Jordan's are you crazy!" the kid answers.

"Dude seriously?" Barry said,

"Hey guys we need to barricade these windows up and quickly," Jordan said taking charge.

"Let's get these mattresses and dressers up against the windows," he ordered.

Barry walked over to the wall phone and hung it up back on its hook, as soon as he did it begin ringing.

"Hello," he answered.

"Who's this?" the voice ask on the other end.

"Barry."

"How old are you Barry?"

"Eleven."

"Listen, Barry, this is the Camp Director, is there anyone older that's in charge right now with you guys?" he asks with a sense of urgency in his voice.

"Jordan when is your birthday?" he shouted across the room.

"June 26, 1976," Jordan shouted back.

"Yes two months older than me," he said.

"Jordan Mr. Flowers wants to speak with you?"

Jordan walked over and took the phone out of Barry's hand while his fellow campers look nervously on.

"Yes," he said.

"Son, what's your name?"

"Jordan."

"Jordan how many of you are in the cabin and is everyone safe?"

"It was eight of us, but one of my friends got dragged out of the cabin by a giant worm," Jordan said distressed.

"What? Sorry to hear that Jordan, but we are going to have to evacuate this area and quick or we all are going to be screwed, do you understand what I am saying to you Son?"

"Yes," Jordan said.

"We are going to bring a bus around in two minutes make sure you get everybody on that bus, do you understand Jordan?"

"Yes, two minutes," Jordan repeated, assuring him that he knew the directive he had just given him.

"Listen, everyone, grab your stuff and take the barriers down from the doors we are leaving by bus in two minutes," Jordan shouted out.

Something large from outside slam up against the cabin rattling it from inside, causing the campers inside to brace themselves.

Jordan tried to listen out for that familiar squeal of the bus amongst all the noise and mayhem.

"It's here!" Barry shouted out as he looked out the windows.

"Let's go!' Jordan shouted out to the other campers.

But unknown to the campers bigger problems was headed their way at one hundred and eighty-one miles per hour, four *Apache Helicopters* equipped with 30mm guns and hellfire missiles were en route to obliterating everything within that sector and a two-mile radius of the summer camp.

Their *E.t.a.* was forty minutes and counting.

"Ward you are an asshole," Flowers said.

"You knew all along, but you did not warn us you fuck!"

"Cry me a river won't you? All you need to know is we need to get on that bus and get the hell out of here Flowers!" Dr. Ward stammered as he took a swipe at something large that had flown by his face.

"Fuck you, Ward! not before you help me get those kids and the staff on those buses you asshole," Flowers asserted.

Lead by Jordan the other children started filtering out the cabin and headed towards the bus.

"Hurry up you little shits! Can't you see we are under… Dr. Ward never finishes his sentence because a giant flying palmetto bug scoops him up by the shoulders and flies off with him screaming and dangling in the air.

Flowers look on in shock before a smile comes across his face.

"Have a safe fight you asshole," he says, before turning his attention back to the children.

The flamethrowers are still holding their own with the attacking bugs, but Flowers knows it won't be too long before they run out of fuel and then what? He thinks.

Camp assistant Bethenny covered in bug juice and blood runs up to assist Flowers with loading the children on the bus.

Aaaaaaahhhh! The scream of death turns their attention to one of the flamethrowers that are now being overpowered and covered by Palmetto Bugs bigger than humans.

Jordan is the last one to board the bus when he hears the faint sound of his name being called out amongst the chaos.

"Jordannnn, Jordannnn…"

"Jordan what are you waiting for son? Get on the bus," Flower's said with a sense of urgency in his voice.

"Jordannnn, Jordannnn…" the voice called out to him again which now sound more like moaning to him that couldn't have been by his estimates no more than fifty meters away.

"You don't hear that; I think it's Juice! I'll be right back," Jordan said as he runs over to the dead flamethrower that is being devoured by the mutant palmetto bugs, picks up the flamethrower gun, the one that he is familiar with and takes off in a mad dash towards the direction from which he thinks he heard the voice calling out his name.

"You got five minutes son then we are leaving!" Flowers shout out behind him.

He looks at Bethenny standing next to him on the bus. "Who is Juice?"

"That would be Franklin sir," she answers.

"Oh," he replies.

"Who the hell is Franklin?" he asks.

"Juice where are you?" Jordan shouts out as he searches in the dark for his friend.

"Jordannnn over here help meeee," he hears the voice call out closer now near him.

Jordan sees something that looks like it's all tightly wrapped up in a spider web-like mummy cocoon to him, so he walks over to investigate it.

The mummy coughs, its mouth breaks thru the web, then the words come out startling Jordan.

"Jordan help me."

"Juice!" Jordan blurts out excited and begins ripping thru the webby cocoon, slowly revealing his friend underneath.

He then hears something coming up behind him and fast. Jordan spins around with the flamethrower with his finger on the trigger.

"Jordan No!" shouts his friend Barry.

" What in the hell, Barry? I almost burn the stink off of you!" Jordan said.

"Bro, I thought you'll need this flashlight," Barry said grinning, holding a flashlight in his hand.

He looks down at the ground at the partially unwrapped cocoon.

"Is that Juice?" he asks.

"Yeah give me a hand."

Barry sees it first out of the side of his eye as he helps unwrap his friend, something large with lots of legs moving towards them at lightning speed, a giant spider!

"Jordan watch out!" he shouts.

Jordan spins around again with the flamethrower and presses the trigger, but nothing comes out but the hissing of gas.

"Fuck!" he says to himself.

The giant arachnid is almost upon them and closing in quickly.

"Come on, come on," Jordan said as he shakes the flamethrower.

He can now see the spiders mandibles and multiple black eyes staring down at him like he is dinner.

"Eat this!"

Jordan presses the trigger one more time, and this time a flame of fire shoots out from the nozzle of the thrower engulfing the monstrous arachnid in flames, as it lets out an ear-piercing shrilling sound. Jordan and Barry watch as the creature begins to burn, turns and retreats into the darkness from which it came on its spindly legs engulf in a halo of flames.

"That's right run spider bitch!" Barry yells out.

Juice slowly begins to come out of his cocoon state of inanimation. Jordan and Barry lift him off the ground back onto his feet.

"Homeboys am I ever glad to see yall ugly faces," he said with a smile.

"Likewise Juice, we got to go now," Jordan said.

Juice with the assistance of Jordan and Smith holding him up made a limping run towards the bus.

They could see the yellow school buses were beginning to drive off, leaving all three of them behind.

"No, no, stop, stop!" They all yell at the buses as they ran behind them, trying to catch up.

A shrilling noise came from behind them, and Jordan turn around just in time to see the spider now smoldering in smoke charging towards them.

"Look out!" Barry said as he tackles Jordan and Juice to the ground pushing them out of the way of the bus going back in reverse towards the spider.

Splatttt! The bus collides with the spider, disintegrating it! As the rest of its carcass gets flatten underneath the bus undercarriage and tires.

The bus comes to a screeching halt as the doors fly open.

" You guy needs a ride?" A smiling Bethenny said.

E.t.a. twenty-five minutes and counting.

The bus pulled off, tires squealing leaving dust behind, Camp Firefly behind. And when the buses were two miles outside of Camp Firefly's perimeter hellfire missiles, and 30mm rounds lit up Camp Firefly and every monstrous size creepy crawler and flying abomination like the Fourth of July.

Epilogue

Six years later, the official report was that an explosion had occurred at a nearby chemical plant and that the smoke fumes from it traveling miles in the air had caused possible mass hallucinations at Camp Firefly and may have also been responsible for the arsonist acts carried out at the camp.

There is a saying that if you keep repeating a lie over and over again to the masses, even lies eventually begins to sound like the truth.

Jordan and his brother Michael had grown closer as the years past, and the teasing had stopped as soon as Jordan had come back from Camp Firefly six years ago. Jordan was unaware, but Michael had sensed something immediately had changed about his little brother.

Present day: 1993 Saginaw Michigan

Brothers, Jordan and Michael accompanied by their girlfriends, and a few friends sat around the campfire they had set up, drinking beers and laughing when Michael feels something crawling up his back.

He jumps up from where he is seated. "Shit! There's something on me," he says as he begins shaking the back of his t-shirt.

His group of friends think its funny and begin laughing.

Jordan walks over and reaches under his brother t-shirt and grabs hold of a healthy size wood spider and pulls it off his brothers back.

"Bro, get that thing away from me, that joker is a monster," Michael said rattled.

Jordan then remembers how his big brother Michel use to tease him and call him "Butterfly Bobby" when he was younger. How times have changed since then, he thinks.

" Nahhh, bro, I've seen bigger," Jordan states with confidence, as he tosses the bushy spider back into the woods.

• • •

Samantha Jackson, the investigative reporter for The Night Turner Tribune, was at her desk putting the finishing touches on a story that she had been working on before she had left for New Orleans, on the demonic possession and exorcism of Maria Langelli in Lisle, Illinois.

Sam looked up to see her bosse's secretary approaching her desk.

"Hey Sam, Avery wants to see you in his office," she said.

"Let me finish this up; I'll be there in a sec," Sam inform her.

Sam knocked on Mr. Denton's office door, and as usual, he was on the phone again about something but this time to her surprise he looks pleasantly happy.

"He looks up and sees her thru the door glass pane with his name and title written on it; *Avery Denton Editor in Chief* and waves her in.

"Hey chief I heard you wanted to see me," Sam said.

"Hi Sam, yes I did, please have a seat," he said gesturing towards the chair in front of his desk.

Sam knew anytime Denton told her to have a seat something must be up.

Her question was, what was it this time? She thought.

"By the way Sam, good work on the New Orleans, case."

"Thanks, boss," she said.

'What do you know about Detroit?"

"It's close to Chicago," she said with a smirk.

'I got a case I think you might be interested in that happen at a summer camp up in Petoskey Michigan a while back ago," he said, handing her off the file.

Sam took the file from Denton, open its manilla folder and made a quick scan over a few of the pages.

Giant roaches and mosquitos the size of pelicans, sound like my kind of story," Sam said sarcastically.

"I know, but something happen down there Sam, and I feel the public is not being told the truth.

"Who's my contact person Chief?" Sam ask.

"let me see here Sam," Denton said as he ruffled thru some papers on his desk.

"Oh here we go," he said as he picked up a business card off his desk and handed it to her.

Sam look at the card in her hand.

Major Richard E. Stone, United States Army.

THE END

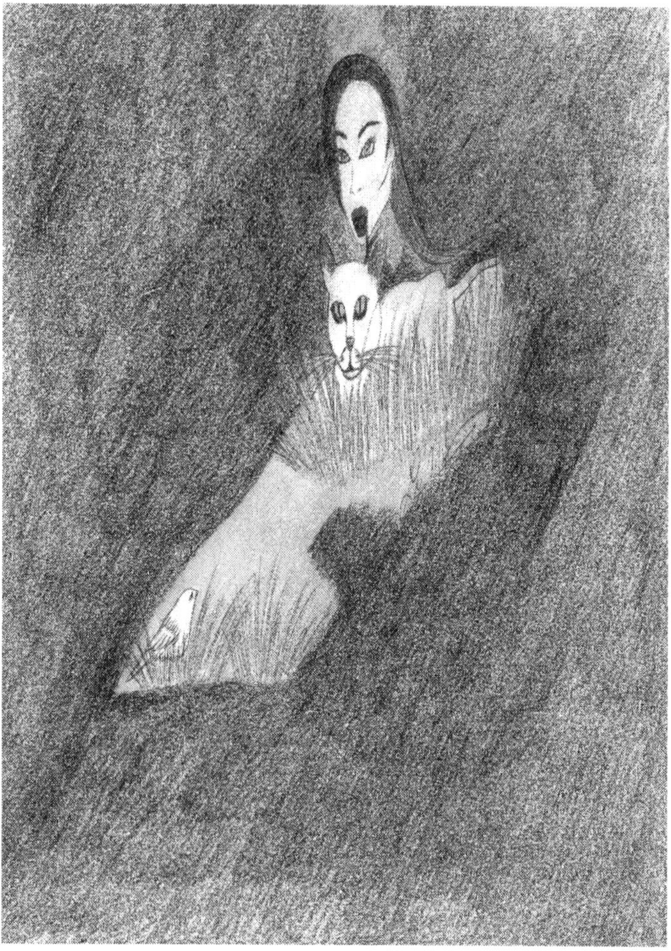

THE COUSIN

ORIGINAL STORY: BY LEE J. MINTER
ARTWORK BY: LEE J. MINTER

Chapter One

God knows I should have listened; I should have paid attention. All the red flags were popping up, like a pan of Jiffy pop popcorn on a hot ass stove. But I just chose to ignore them, ignore the haters, as I like to call them. The jealous family members, the naysayers, my wife.

You see my friend, for you to understand this story, you have to understand my point of view, how I was not thinking about what other people no matter how close to me, was trying to tell me about the cousin I grew up with, the cousin I thought I knew, but in truth was never known.

We all make mistakes, that's why when my cousin Alyson Webb who had just got parole from doing a two year bid up at Folsom State Prison in Califonia, had asked if she could stay with us for a little while until she could find a job and a place of her own.

Aaaahhh, you say? How sweet of me you say. Please save the sentiment for someone else that better deserves it more, my friend.

"Because I believe it was my mother that first introduce me to the phrase, "The road to hell is paved with good intentions."

I had without hesitation and against my better judgment said yes to her so that she could have some place to stay, someplace to lay her head not around strangers but with family.

After all isn't prison suppose to be a place of rehabilitation? That was a debate I had with my wife, Hallie constantly.

"Give her a chance," I said to myself.

"To prove herself?," I proposed strongly.

"It's not what you think," trying to believe the voice in my head.

Someone once said it's not easy to sleep with one eye open when you have someone in your house that is capable of any and everything.

Guess what? That, someone, was absolutely on point and unapologetically correct.

But if insomnia had been the least of my worries my friend, I tell you I would not be writing this story.

We all make mistakes, my name is Dustin Farmer, and my mistake was not listening to my wife, my family members, and my friends. No, let me reword this, *my big ass mistake* was the day I allowed my cousin Alyson Webb back into my life.

But don't listen to me my friend read on and judge for yourself that is why I title this cautionary tale - "The Cousin."

CHAPTER TWO

Where do I begin my story? That's easy; it would start on the day I pick my cousin up at the Folsom Correctional Facility Prisoner visiting center, the day she was parole from custody, with the clothes on her back and the shoes on her feet literally.

My wife and my young son Josh accompanied me reluctantly might I add, to pick her up from the visiting center of the Correctional Facility.

I was informed earlier by the prison officials if I did not arrive there in a timely fashion, that Alyson would be taken in a prison van and drop off at the nearest Greyhound Bus Station or Amtrak Train Station and given fare to get back home courtesy of the California Department of Corrections (CDCR).

Bottom line once she was released, she was no longer their problem until she fucks up again, so I made it my business to get my ass there early so she would not have to enjoy the comforts of their escort to her return back to what they call in prison "the world."

Alyson who I should mention is my first cousin on my Farther's brother side. I have to say by all appearances she seemed to be one of those that did prison and did not let prison do her if you get my drift. She had all her worldly possessions in what look like a laundry bag and a beaming smile on her face when she greeted us outside.

Not too long after exchanging nice falsities about how good all of us look and awkward hugs, we all loaded up in the family van and proceeded back home to Scottsdale Arizona. A long drive back home that with a few interchanges of pleasantries between us adults it was mostly a trip back home filled with silence.

That is until my eleven-year-old inquisitive son Josh, ask his Aunt Alyson, the embarrassing question " Aunt Alyson was you a "stud" in prison or a "femme?" he asked.

"Ambidextrous," she replied laughing and much to our amazement. Needless to say, the ride got much quieter on the way back, while my son googled up the definition of ambidextrous and had this strange grin on his face that I could see thru the rearview mirror.

Was my Josh just curious, dumb, or both?, or maybe as I stated earlier just inquisitive.

Maybe I should have been more inquisitive, or maybe the apple doesn't fall too far from the tree, excuse the metaphor.

But enough of the self-introspective, I know you're wondering what the hell did Alyson do that cost her three years of her life in prison.

I call it blind love but the court and state call it embezzlement and stealing any sum of money over one thousand precious dollars from your employer especially if you are on probation can get you that amount of time and then some.

In her case, it was over fifty thousand dollars from a real estate company she worked for right underneath her Boss nose while she was fucking him behind his wife's back, and feeding her boyfriend's cocaine habit at the same time.

We all make mistakes as I said. And my cousin had done her time even got an associate's degree while in prison and had discovered Christ from what she told me in her numerous letters.

I had pointed out all her accomplishments to my wife Hallie and even put her on an ideological pedestal as an example of when prison reform actually works for the betterment of a convicted felony's life.

I ignored all the past rumors and innuendos mostly thru family members that my cousin Alyson was unnaturally attracted to me and could be a very manipulative and controlling person.

The thought that her displays of affection were nothing more than familial never cross my mind until she crossed the line.

Family members I rationalize are just jealous of our relationship because now Alyson is trying to get back on her feet and I am the one supporting her in her effort.

"You are my favorite cousin," Alyson would constantly tell me.

At that time I had no idea what she meant. But I would soon find out.

We had even addressed those salacious family rumors.

"Nonsense," she said.

"What's up with those kissy face emojies your cousin is texting you? Don't you think that's inappropriate?" My wife Hallie asked me, long before Alyson got incarcerated.

"I know it seems strange baby, but I don't think she means anything about that," I said.

"And xoxoxo," my wife asked.

"Don't that mean I love you?" I said.

What was I waiting for you ask? A fucking piano to fall on my head from out of the sky like in the cartoons.

A lesson learned, a lesson lived they say.

Hey, but Alyson was here and goddamit we were going to make the best of it until she moves on to other arrangements that her parole officer according to her was making for her transition back into our world.

"I don't want to impose," she said.

"Not all Alyson you're family," I assured her with a smile.

I showed Alyson her new room that was slightly off to the left not far from her nephew, Josh. It was a full bathroom in the middle of the two rooms that separated them apart from each other.

"Wow it's been a long time since I've slept on a real mattress, I am going to sleep like a baby," she said, kissing me lightly on my cheek.

"Good to have you home Alyson," I said.

She looked at me and smiled and went into her room.

But I could not help wonder what her life must have been like for Alyson while she was incarcerated.

Three years spent in one of the toughest prisons in California I thought, as I made my way back to the comforts of my bedroom.

Little did I know Alyson did not have to get ready for Folsom prison before she went in. Folsom prison had to get ready for Alyson Webb.

Red Flag number one.

Chapter Three

Josh stood up at the crack doorway of the hallway bathroom with his mouth hanging open as he watched his Aunt Alyson standing naked in front of the bathroom sink brushing her teeth.

But what had his attention was the tattoo on her back of the whining snake that appears to slither down her backside with its head going down to her buttocks, its serpent tongue flickering right out between the crease of her cheeks.

"Josh?" I shouted out as I came out of my bedroom and seen him standing in the hall.

Josh just looked at me and pointed at the bathroom door.

I walked over and was just as stun as my son, it was obvious that Alyson had been working out and had the goods to prove it. I did not think it was appropriate; it was now on full display in front of my young son.

"Alyson the door," I said getting her attention.

"Oh I am sorry it must have come open," she said looking at our surprise faces as she closes the door.

I shook my head sideways not sure what to make out of what I just saw.

"Son go use the guest bathroom downstairs will ya," I told him.

"Oh' that's right we do have one downstairs," Josh said slightly embarrassed, but with a hint of sarcasm that I found annoying giving the circumstances.

"Yeah, I don't think it moved overnight," I assured him.

• • •

When Hallie got a hold of what had happened, she hit the roof. I have to admit the possibility that Alyson had left the door cracked open intentionally because she wanted us to see her in her birthday suit did not sit well with me either.

But just for peace of mind and to quiet my wife concerns, I check the hinges on the upstairs hall bathroom door, and to my surprise, they did seem a little stiff to me, so I applied a little WD-40 lubricant to both hinges, and the door appeared to shut more easily.

That revelation offered my wife Hallie some relief, but only to a certain degree, might I add.

It was still an awkward breakfast the three of us had that morning together, and I could see the wheels of curiosity turning in my son's head before he opened his mouth to take another bite of his bacon.

"So Aunt Alyson how long have you had that snake tattoo?" he asked.

"Josh do you think that's …" his mother interrupted before Alyson interjected.

"No it's quite okay, I got it while I was in prison," Alyson answer.

"Wow, It's badass," my son said, obviously impressed.

"Josh watch the language," my wife corrected him.

"Thanks, Josh," Alyson said as her eyes went over to me.

I could not tell if she was trying to read my face to see if I felt the same way as my son? So, therefore, I maintain a poker face as if I had no stake in the game.

I look at my watch, saved by the bell I thought. "Josh eat up, or you are going to miss your bus for school," I said.

"Any big plans today Cuz?" I said. More than happy to take the conversation in another direction.

"Just the usual ex-convict stuff, make contact with my parole officer and start looking for some work," she said.

"Sounds like a plan," I said, trying to sound as optimistic as possible.

"Do you need any extra cash?" I ask.

"Thanks, but I am good, go fix some teeth Doc," she said.

"Oh' by the way I apologize for this morning guys, I did not know the bathroom door was open," Alyson said with what sounded like to me genuine remorse in her voice.

"Don't worry about it Cuz, the only problem is Josh might want to get himself a snake tattoo," I said as my son had left the table by now and was headed off to school.

Hallie gave me that look as she took another sip of her coffee.

"Enjoy your day at work baby, I'll talk to you later," my wife said, as she kissed me on my cheek.

"Thanks,' I said relieved in a selfish way that I had a valid reason (work) for not having to be around my cousin after that uncomfortable exposition of herself this morning, intentional or unintentional.

And it definitely did not help that I still had that image of her embarassedly in my head.

Maybe some time alone with Alyson I thought, would be good for Hallie to maybe bond with her or get to know her better, after all, she was her cousin n law, and she would be staying with us until she made her transition into her "own" place.

The day went fairly well at my dentist office except for the numerous calls and interruptions from Alyson to see how my day was going. I rack it up to being that she was very grateful that we were letting her stay with us and that's how she was expressing or showing her gratitude.

I thought I was overreacting to her numerous calls until my fellow resident dentist and friend Allen, asked me jokingly if I was cheating on Hallie, because of all the phone interruptions.

I tried to put it nicely to Alyson as possible, that I was busy at the office with my patients and if it wasn't important to please leave a message at the desk with one of my receptionist.

I also wonder though, if she was busy with my wife who had the day off from work that day. How in the hell did she have time to call me this much at work? Heck' my wife Hallie didn't even call me this much unless it was something of the utmost importance.

Maybe, I was overreacting, not taking into account Alyson had just gotten out of prison, and her behavior was probably nothing more than anxiety and stress from just getting released. Maybe I should give her a few days to whine down I concluded.

It was a long day, and I was looking forward to getting home. I look at my incoming phone calls on my cars interactive display screen, good there were no more phone calls from my cousin.

The scent of roast beef and potatoes and baked jalapeno cornbread instantly hit my nose as I entered my house.

"Wow, something smells good," I said as I made my way upstairs to shower before dinner.

"Hi there cousin," Alyson said to me as she descended the stairs in a white top that was so tight you could almost see her nipples and some daisy duke shorts that looked like they were painted on her ass.

"Hey Alyson," I said with what must have been a bewildered look on my face as I made my way upstairs.

Was this the same cousin looking like she was going to a white trash rodeo that said she had discovered Christ?

Hallie greeted me and was not far behind me as I made my way up into our room.

"What the hell is she wearing?" my wife lit into me.

"How the hell am I suppose to know, she's been with you all day," I said back to Hallie, I was tired and just wanted to take a shower and sink my teeth into some of that roast beef and potatoes.

"Look I took her to the mall, but I did not know she was going to buy them hoe clothes," Hallie said.

"Shhhhh, she might hear you," I said.

"I don't care if she does, that bitch is going to have to find another house to walk around half naked," my wife said frustrated.

"If I can cover my ass up and this is my house you don't think I am going to tolerate Ms. loosey-goosey out there do you?" My wife protested, her arms folded with the most serious look on her face that I had not seen in a very long time.

"Hallie calm down, I'll talk to her," I assured my wife.

"You better we got an eleven-year-old son, and Ms. Nasty is not going to be walking around here like like this, is the red light district," my pissed off wife said.

"Shhhh, I got this," I said trying to calm my wife down.

As I watched my wife storm out of our bedroom, I had to agree that she was right. It wasn't like Alyson was a teenager we were talking about dressing so provocative; this was a woman that was forty-one years old six years my senior.

High school was over a long time ago.

I made my way down to dinner after taking a nice hot shower and to my surprise guess what? Alyson had changed into a more conservative knee-length flower print dress, had she heard our argument upstairs I wonder? Or did she realize the clothes she had on was just a little to scuzzy for my wife taste, excuse me our taste? I wonder what had motivated her from dressing like a teenager's wet dream? To like she was hosting a Tupperware party now. I took a seat at the dining room table.

"Nice dress Alyson," I said.

"Thanks, I was feeling a little uptight about what I had on," she said.

"Excuse me?" I said detecting a possible underlying message in her remark.

'Nevermind Dustin, just because you got it don't mean you have to flaunt it right Hallie?" She said.

"That depends on who you are flaunting it to," my wife answer as she dispenses us all healthy portions of roast beef and potatoes on our plates.

"Amen," Alyson said winking at me, catching me off guard.

"Flaunting what?" my son Josh asks.

"Nevermind," I said to him.

"Let me give you a hand with dinner Hallie," my cousin offers, as she got up from the table and brought over a bowl of biscuits.

'That would be great," Hallie said.

Alyson to all of our surprise said a nice prayer before dinner, and we all ate.

Hallie seemed more relaxed at dinner. Afterward, I help her clean and put up the dishes while Alyson gave Josh a hand with his homework outside on the patio terrace, which gave Hallie and me the opportunity to talk in private finally.

"I guess whatever you told her must have worked," she said looking at me.

"Told her what? I thought you talk to her," I said.

"No I did not," Hallie said handing me off one of the dishes she rinsed off which I then put in the dishwasher.

"You think she heard us?" I said.

"Maybe," Hallie replied.

"What other reason would account for her sudden change in fashion," she said.

"Do you think we owe her an apology?" I said.

"Of course not. We don't want Alyson to think it's okay for her to parade herself around our house half-naked unless you're comfortable with that Dustin?"

"Of course not," I said to my wife.

"Maybe you want me to put on some booty shorts?" Hallie said.

"I would like that very much Mrs. Farmer," I teased her giving my wife a smooch on the lips.

"Old pervert," my wife said slapping me with the dish towel.

I laughed and went in for another kiss and some tickles.

"Let's make some margarita's tonight," Hallie proposed.

"Sounds good to me," I said.

That night after we all had retired to bed, I had the strangest dream that Alyson and I were walking together with her ex-boyfriend Markus when suddenly she fell to the ground and begin to have a seizure.

Markus stood there watching in silence almost detach as I attempted to offer aid to my cousin.

As I placed my hands on her shoulder screaming for help, she suddenly came to and grabbed me by the testicles, her eyes rolled back in her head, and I could only see the whites of her sclera as she begins licking my neck with her wet tongue, a snakes tongue.

I called out her name and screamed at her to let go of my balls, but it was almost like she had a death grip on them as she started crushing them.

"Alyson stop!" And then I woke up. I check my balls, and yes they appeared to be still intact thank God. I looked over at my wife Hallie, and she was still fast asleep. What the hell did that dream mean, I thought as I got out of the bed to go to the bathroom to get a glass of water, although I required something stiffer to put me back to sleep after that dream from hell.

After I had used the bathroom, I heard a noise downstairs like the television was on. I looked over at the clock on our nightstand; it was 2:00 am in the morning. Who the hell could be up at this time in the morning, I thought as I made my way slowly down the stairs to the living room. I could see the reflection of the light from the television bouncing off the walls as I got closer to the living room, and I could also hear the sounds of someone having sex in the living room on the television.

I stood there in awe as I watch her in disbelief, as Alyson sat on my sofa with her legs spread apart masturbating to hardcore porn on my television screen.

The male stud on the screen pounded the female porn star from behind into oblivion as she yelled out profanity-laced request to her male counterpart.

• • •

My eyes went back to my cousin, softly moaning as she pleasures herself, unaware of my presence in the room or was she?

Red Flag number two, she would have to go and soon I concluded.

Chapter Four

I was too embarrassed and ashamed to tell my wife Hallie what I had borne witness to that night in our living room on our sofa. After all, how could I ever justify bringing a person like my cousin Alyson that had so blatantly disrespected our home and taken my kindness for weakness back into our lives with her bullshit? I couldn't.

It was obvious to me that Alyson was sick and needed some mental health treatment. Contrary to that Hallie and I had an eleven-year-old son, and I could not in good conscience allow this kind of sickness around our little boy.

Alyson apologized for her behavior all the way to the halfway house for her obscene conduct and appeared to show genuine displays of remorse and embarrassment for her actions at my family's home.

On the flip side of that coin, I felt genuine relief when I drop her ass off at her new digs and an even bigger one knowing that I and my family lives could return to some sense of normalcy again.

Alyson name only came up again when my wife she got the cable bill and reviewed the bill and saw that a hardcore porn movie call *The Rough Riders* had been purchased.

I explain to her that I had caught Alyson watching that movie, but I never told her what I had seen, and my wife never asked.

• • •

Six years had now passed by with no word or contact from my cousin Alyson when one day I got a call at work from her asking if I was okay with meeting her at a nearby restaurant for lunch.

Alyson explained to me that she had been wrestling with all kind of demons when she had got out of prison and was sincerely sorry for the way that she had shown her gratitude when we had open our home to her six years ago.

She only wanted our forgiveness and for us to see that she had not been a lost cause after all.

After speaking with my wife Hallie about it, I agreed to meet Alyson on a pleasant sunny day at one of the local cafes nearby my office.

To my surprise, I hardly recognize the person that walked up to me that day that was my cousin Alyson. She was very conservative and professionally dressed and gave me a friendly hug before we sat down at our table at the small café.

I instantly notice the wedding ring on her finger and congratulated her on her marriage.

Did I feel slighted that I had not the wedding? Under the circumstances, not in the least.

" JT is a handsome man Dustin. I cannot wait for you to meet him," she said.

Alyson explained to me how she had gone back to school and had obtained her master's degree in religious education and that she and JT had now started a small ministry in the San Diego area, but it was still growing.

She seemed sincere in the change that she had made and I it appeared that some great metamorphosis had taken place in her life. Was it divinity from God or some other force? I was not qualified to answer that question.

But I was happy for her and told her I was proud of her accomplishments, over corn beef sandwiches and potato chips.

It had been after all six years since the last time I had seen my cousin Alyson Webb.

Alyson gave me her business card with a long name of her organization on it the "*Ministries of the Enlighten ones*" right before we said our goodbyes to each other.

We parted ways after wishing each other the best of luck in the café that day.

I thought that would be the last time I would see Alyson for a while; I was wrong.

"Hey, baby how was your day?" I said to my wife Hallie as I enter the house.

"Perfect," she said kissing me on the lips.

"By the way thanks for the beautiful bouquet of flowers you sent me," she said.

"What flowers?" I said clueless.

"These honey," she said pointing to the ones on the dining room table in the vase.

They were beautiful, and they look expensive, but I hated to burst her bubble they did not come from me.

Hallie walked over to the bouquet just as befuddled as I was and picked up the gift card that I assumed she never read implanted inside the vase.

"From Alyson and JT best wishes to the Farmers," she said.

"Who's JT?" she asked.

"Her husband," I said.

"Alyson?" my wife responded surprise.

"Yes," I said almost unable to maintain my composure.

"Freaky Alyson?" Hallie ask again as if she heard me wrong the first time.

"Yes babe and freaky Alyson is now a minister," I said with a straight face that was starting to crack from holding in laughter.

"A minister to who? A bunch of rough riders," my wife said.

I burst out laughing at my wife response no longer able to hold it in, as I walked over and grabbed two cold beers out of the fridge.

I open both of them and hand my wife one.

"She said she turn her life around, went back to school and got her masters degree in theology," I said.

"Do tell."

"Yep, and married the man of her dreams and now they've started a ministry somewhere down in San Diego."

"I'll be damn," my wife said, taking a sip of her cold beer.

"I guess that saying is true," Hallie said.

"What's that?" I answered.

"The Lord works in mysterious ways," she said.

"I guess he does," I agreed, taking a sip of my cold beer. But in the back of my mind, I could not forget the devil also does my friend, the devil also does.

CHAPTER FIVE

Several weeks had passed my friend before I heard from my cousin Alyson again when she called and invited my family and me down to a service at her church in San Diego. I wanted to decline graciously, but something inside of me wanted to give her the benefit of the doubt that she had changed her life around.

She deserved one more chance at redemption. Not that it was mine to give that is. I did not want to be one of those people that believe people could not change for the better if they honestly tried.

Furthermore, I had felt slightly guilty that church or a religious service had not been a part of my family's busy lives in a while. That being said, I had to practically twist Josh's arm to go with us that evening, to weird Auntie Alyson's church service.

He was right the service was weird, it was about ten people altogether that attended that service, and the three of us made up that ten in a small little building in San Diego. But I got the impression that Alyson was doing something that she loved, and at least I had made an effort to show up and give my support.

JT her husband for the most part was a polite and unusual quite man who I got the impression played whatever role Alyson required of him in their lives, her dominance over him in their relationship was obvious by the way she talked to him which made all of us all slightly uncomfortable over dinner, to say the least.

I remember her complimenting "JT" when we had lunch together weeks ago, but now I saw none of that display of affection over the course of our meal. The man appeared to be afraid of voicing his opinion about anything we discussed that evening, and if he did have something to say, Alyson would cut him down like a Ginsu knife in her quest to control the narrative of the conversation.

I begin to wonder if Alyson had changed. Her and my wife never interacted much that evening except a few cordial exchanges of pleasantries between them. And every time Josh looked at her I was wondering was he still thinking about the snake tattoo whining down her back to her buttocks? In short, we were all glad when the evening ended, and we said our goodbyes and I doubted very much if we would be seeing my cousin Alyson anytime soon.

I would be wrong.

A few days later Alyson and her husband JT popped up at our house uninvited, explaining that they were just in the neighborhood and wanted to drop by and say hello, not wanting to be rude Hallie and I invited them in and entertained our company while trying to hide our displeasure for their surprise visit.

Alyson was her domineering self, and JT sat their quietly like the cat got his tongue literally, hanging on to every word silently that came out of Alyson's mouth like a trapeze artist.

But if he did attempt to speak Alyson would cut him a look that would instantly send him into a quiet mode where he would pout like a small child.

It was a spectacle to behold that made me and Hallie completely uncomfortable.

By the time they had left Alyson had gone thru two whole bottles of our most expensive wine and gave us the impression that she would have started working on a third bottle if we allowed it.

Her tolerance and consumption were impressive, and she seemed to have no sense of timing when it was appropriate to leave our home that evening.

Hallie and I both had to work that following morning and had to start displaying signs of exhaustion before Alyson, and her husband finally departed.

By then the both of us were mentally exhausted and physically drained, and I know this sounds rude, but we promise each other if those two ever showed up like that again uninvited, regardless if we were at home we would not answer the door.

The phone calls started back up again at work from Alyson, and despite my declarations to her that I was busy, she seemed to show no regard for my personal time, and space and her phone calls and text messages increased in their capacity.

My wife Hallie started to get mysterious calls at the house, but when she would answer the phone, whoever was calling would say nothing and then hang up.

Hallie, my wife, offered to speak with her about these unnerving disruptions in our life but I told her to give it some time maybe Alyson will go away if I ignore her because I did not want to rock the boat.

The wrong answer my friend because unknown to me at that time, the more you ignore some people, the more they become preoccupied and obsess with you.

Guess what? Alyson was one of those people.

They also say with stalkers, rejection builds obsession, which I should have taken heed of my friend because a wrecking ball was coming my way.

And it was up to me to get the hell out of its path.

Red Flag number three.

Alyson's daily and consistent disruptions in my family lives had now become more than just mere annoyances to now outright harassment. The final straw that had broken the camel's back excuse the cliché was when she called me at work and started drilling me in regards to why I had not returned her calls.

Believe it or not, she even dared to ask me when we planned on visiting her cult-like church again? I had a one-word answer for that, *never.*

But what mess me up in the head was when she told me that even though we were cousins, she had been given a vision by God that we belonged together and that anyone that stood in the way of that would have hell to pay.

I could not believe that she had just threatened the ones I loved and me, besides disrespecting my marriage to Hallie.

I informed Alyson as calmly as I could, despite the not so subtle threat I had just received from my cousin, that she was confused and what she was saying to me was wrong on so many levels.

I suggested to her that I thought she needed psychiatric help and that she and JT might want to get themselves into some counseling. But her next words to me was just as stunning as her first and took me completely by surprise and off guard.

"You did not think that I needed help that night Dustin when I was on your sofa, and you were watching me, enjoying the show you fucking little freak," she said.

"What's wrong Dustin? Cats got your tongue," she taunted me.

"Do Hallie know what kind of pervert she has for a husband?" she continues on, obviously enjoying her onslaught of insults towards my character and reputation as a father and a husband.

"No, but she knows what kind of bitch that I have for a cousin!" I shouted into the phone now mad as hell.

"Fuck you!" She said and hung up the phone.

The feelings that she had just expressed in the end was amicable, to say the least, and I now speculated whether or not I should take out a restraining order on a cousin that was unstable. And once again, I decided against my better judgment my friend, to take a more diplomatic approach after discussing my options with Hallie.

I decided to give her husband JT a call, under the assumption that maybe he was not aware of what was going on, and maybe we could work something out and get his wife the help she needed. Instead, I ran into a brick wall.

JT told me he had heard from his wife earlier in their relationship, about me. "That I was the cousin that had amorous feelings for his wife and I was the one stalking her and better back off." And if I persisted with my lies and allegations that I would be hearing from their attorney soon for my slanderous and unfounded accusations against the stellar reputation that his wife had now earned for herself in their community.

It took all I had to keep the bile from coming up from my stomach and out of my mouth listening to this horse shit.

He then had the audacity to tell me. "That the only reason that Alyson had invited my family and me to their church, was because she believed every soul needs saving including ours."

The nerve of that arrogant bastard I thought. Could he not see that Alyson was using him? Just like she had used everybody else that had the misfortune of crossing her path.

I did not know if the man was an enabler, a victim or a fool? Or all three. But it was obvious that Alyson was the one calling the shots in their relationship, and maybe he was just a co-conspirator to her madness.

I told JT "He was wrong on all accounts and that he had the real story all twisted, from the lies that his wife had fed him, to the lies that he was now feeding me." The phone went dead silent, proceeded by a dial tone, as I marveled at how well our conversation went.

That goes to show you that you can't rationalize with a grown ass man when he's pussy whip, titty fed and hypnotize, not necessarily in that order, I might add.

If he were sitting in my dentist chair, I'd pull out wisdom teeth that he didn't have without local anesthesia.

Chapter Six

A week had now gone by without any contact made by my cousin Alyson, and it was a welcoming relief to myself and my family, and we were all able to rest a little more better.

Maybe her husband JT had taken my advice after all I thought and went and got his wife some help, and check himself into counseling while he was at it.

All of my family and me had retired for the night, and we all felt we could sleep more comfortably with the new alarm system that we had recently installed because of Alyson's threats and stalking behavior. Like I said we all thought. It was 2:00 am in the morning when something woke me up out of my sleep, and I went downstairs to investigate.

2:00 am in the morning again, it sounded like someone had left the television on, as I made my way down the stairs slowly towards the living room.

That is when I heard what sounded like the sounds of someone having sex again in my living room, but like the first time, it was coming from the television. Once again, I stared mortified at the tv screen of the same male porno actor pounding the same female porno actress from behind as she yelled the same profanity-laced sexual demands out to him.

Déjà vu.

"Hallie call the police!" I yelled upstairs to my wife.

"What?" I heard my wife yell back downstairs with the sound of fear in her voice.

"Call the police!" I yelled back upstairs again.

I noticed that the upper deck patio light was on and the sliding door appeared to be slightly open as I made my way to it.

I took one of the hanging cooking pots off of the overhead rack for a weapon as I made my way slowly towards the door. And that is when I saw her my cousin Alyson Webb sitting on my patio deck in what look like her nightgown drinking a beer from a six-pack at my fucking table, on my fucking patio deck.

"Excuse the language my friend, but suffice to say I was mad as hell."

"Hey Cuz what's up?" she said in a cheerful voice like I was happy to see her and I had invited her ass over, two nots in a row.

"What the hell do you think you are doing Alyson? You need to leave and now!" I said furiously.

"What does it look like I am doing? I am having a cold beer, that was a long fucking climb up Cuz, and I am thirsty and sweaty," she said nonchalantly.

"You are trespassing Alyson, and I can also have you arrested for breaking into my house, do you understand?" I said pointing at my patio slide door.

"Not even mentioning you are also in violation of the PPO that we have against you," I added.

Alyson laughed at me before she answered back like it was all a big joke.

"Fuck your screen door and Fuck your PPO, Dustin," she said.

"I am going to school you real quick cousin; there are only three kinds of people that put out PPO's where I come from," she said, as she took a swig of her beer.

"And what kind of people are those Alyson," I said, falling into her trap.

"Punks, Pussies, and Old women, cousin," she answers laughing so hard she spit out some of her beer.

"You get it PPO," she said.

"Yeah clever, now leave," I said bluntly.

She blatantly ignores me; I see that this is not going to be easy.

"You like the movie I put on? It's our favorite," she said with a mischievous grin on her face.

I look into Alyson's eye's, and I can now see for the first time, something's not quite right, up there in her head.

"What's going on Dad?" I heard a voice say from behind me.

I turn around it was Josh.

"Go back to bed son its okay," I said.

And that's all it took was that split second when I took my eye off of Alyson I heard my son scream.

"Dad look out!"

Right before I felt the seven-inch butcher knife plunge into my shoulder blade cutting thru my flesh that my cousin Alyson had been concealing all along.

Her ferocious attack and assault with the knife drove me back against the kitchen wall, out of the patio doorway. I instantly reached up and grabbed her hand with the knife as I attempted to wrestle it away from her after she had withdrawn the blade from out of my shoulder and went in for another attack. Alyson twisted the knife towards my hand cutting it, and I instantly drew my slice hand back in pain, any closer, and she would have severed my thumb.

Blood was gushing out of my wounds, and I could tell I was losing a lot of it in my struggle as I start to feel faint.

"Aunt Alyson no! Josh scream out again.

Alyson turned to look at my son.

I took a wild swing at her, and to my surprise, the pot made contact with her head, the blow stun her! Knocking her off balance and a few feet off of me, but she was able to recover quickly and came charging at me again full speed, screaming like a lunatic with the knife held high above her head.

I braced myself for another attack, but I was getting weaker by the minute from blood loss, as my eyes shot straight to the shiny blade in her hand with my blood and flesh already dripping on it and about to get some more.

As she went in for the attack, someone hit Alyson hard from the waist down tackling her as they both went crashing thru the patio screen door. At first, I thought it was my son Josh, but no, my wife Hallie had come out of nowhere and quickly rush her catching her by surprise, and now had Alyson pin down on the patio deck wrestling for the knife wrestling for her life.

Alyson was able to get my wife off her with an elbow to her jaw, that sent Hallie toppling over.

My son Josh instinctively rushed over to protect his mom and was quickly met by a foot to his chest by

Alyson that sent him flying back thru the busted patio doors onto the kitchen floor. He had underestimated Alyson her three years in Folsom had not been wasted; she was not only deadly but quick. Not far behind, I gain my composure and stumble over, feeling lightheaded but I had to defend my family, and I wasn't stopping until I was dead.

I almost got my wish.

Alyson's knife came within an inch of my throat's jugular vein before I was able to react and evade her attack.

By this time my wife had recovered, taking advantage of Alyson's focus on me, Hallie quickly went in for the attack with a Tyson-like punch to Alyson's jaw that sent her over the deck's balcony and sprawled out on our back lawn KO cold.

"Crazy fucking bitch!"

"Don't fuck with my family," Hallie said, spitting down at her.

That day I could have never been prouder of my wife, Hallie.

"Police!" yelled a voice in the distant. "Of course," I said, and then I faded out.

Chapter Seven

Alyson was now facing the possibility of going back to prison after she had been admitted to the hospital for psychiatric evaluation while in custody and under the watchful eye of the Maricopa County Sheriff's Office.

The apologies could not have come quick enough from her husband JT who swore up and down that he had no idea of the seriousness of how deep his wife's mental illness ran, and she had been deceiving him and hiding it from him all the time.

I wanted to tell him that "If a sandwich, smell and taste like a shit sandwich, then guess what?" But I chose to be a little more diplomatic and told him no hard feelings, and I wish him the best of luck, God knows he would be needing it and then some.

As our wounds healed and the days passed turning into weeks, the police and courts told us that they would be contacting us for Alyson's court dates. That was good enough for me, being that I was trying to put this whole sordid affair of events behind us, and move on.

Hallie, Josh and I decided no better way to really put this behind us, was to hold a football viewing party at our home for some family members and friends.

It was a nice turn out that day at our home as we all sat around eating football food and watching the Arizona Cardinals play the Chicago Bears.

Arizona and Chicago were in their fourth quarter possibly going into overtime.

"Hey Hallie, you guys got any more of those pretzels and cheese dip?" our friend Tyrone ask.

"You finish with that second bowl already," Hallie said joking with Tyrone.

"What the hell is that noise?" my sister n law Katy asks.

"Turn the tv down," I said.

We could all hear it now; it sounded like something fast and loud approaching the side of the house.

"Get out of the living room now!" I scream to everyone, only seconds before an ambulance came crashing thru the wall of my front living room, demolishing everything in its path.

"What the fuck!" Tyrone said dropping his fresh bowl of pretzels and dip.

Scottsdale police were right behind the ambulance sirens blaring.

It appeared that someone at the hospital had forgotten to give us a call and warn us that Alyson Webb had overpowered a police officer, escaped custody and was now en route to crash our football party and kill us all.

No thanks to them no one was seriously injured that day, and everyone got out of the living room just in the nick of time to have our asses still attach to our bodies.

Alyson exited the banged-up ambulance in her hospital robe, looked directly at me wild-eyed, smiled and mumble the words "Cuz." Right before Scottsdale police lit her world up with 100,000 volts from their Tasers.

Tyrone looked over at me.

"Man I know you told me you had a crazy ass cousin, but damn."

By the way, just for the record, the Arizona Cardinals won that day.

• • •

Two years had now passed by since our last contact, but I will never forget the cousin that terrorize my family and our home.

Bringgg, bringgg, bringggggg.

Please excuse me while I get the phone.

Operator: *"Arizona State Hospital, will you accept a call from Alyson Webb."*

Click, dial tone.

THE END

Or is it?

LEE J. MINTER

IN SHEEP'S CLOTHING

LEE J. MINTER

THE NIGHT TURNER TRIBUNE

Five Tales Of Terror

SAMANTHA JACKSON

Follow me on Twitter
@LJMHorror4u

Follow me on Instagram
@mintboogie

Visit me @ my web page at
LJMHorrorTales4u.com

IN SHEEP'S CLOTHING
IN SHEEP'S CLOTHING
LEE J. MINTER
LEE J. MINTER

LEE J. MINTER is back again this time with an anthology of five horror and suspense stories to scare the living daylights out of you. Make a hole and make it wide for the new master and self-proclaimed rock star of horror aka mintboogie. Horror will never be the same, stay tuned.

90022558R00163

Made in the USA
San Bernardino, CA
05 October 2018